PHARMA
MAFIA

PHARMA MAFIA

LAWRENCE DRAKE

A Note to the Reader

Please note that this is a novel meant for adults. There is inappropriate language, sex scenes, and references to drugs and violence. If you are uncomfortable with that, this book is not for you.

ISBN Paperback: 978-0-692-68953-0
ISBN Hardcover: 978-0-692-68954-7
ISBN eBook: 978-0-9975242-9-1

Library of Congress Number: 2016938425

Printed in the United States of America

Book Cover Design: Michelle Manley
Interior Design: Ghislain Viau

To my parents – thanks to their encouragement and the belief they instilled in me to never stop pursuing a worthy project.

Table of Contents

 # ONE

The cold, winter moon cast long shadows in the parking lot of a famous restaurant near the Lodge of Four Seasons in southern Missouri. As the half-empty lot suggested, it was off-season at Lake of the Ozarks and would remain so until the following May. But tonight was a special occasion that happened once every four months: It was Chalk Pharmaceuticals' district meeting, which was on its second day at the Lodge.

Vehicles trickled in and their drivers, dressed in business casual, hurried into the restaurant to escape the winter chill. A Pontiac Grand Prix arrived last, but instead of parking with the cluster of cars near the front, the driver slowed to a stop in the far back corner, so secluded that not even the lamplight could reach it.

The passenger-side door opened and a man stepped out.

"Better you park here, away from the rest," he advised. "Don't wanna risk dinging this baby!"

The driver got out of the car.

"Sure is dark. I don't know why anyone else would park back this far," she replied.

They walked toward the restaurant, and the moonlight revealed the driver to be Beth Beacon, dressed to accentuate her positive attitude and great figure. Bright, brunette, and beautiful, Beth was the newest addition to the team and was on the up-and-up, as her shiny company car attested.

Her passenger, or rather, her boss, Chuck Frazier, was everything Beth was not—short, squat, middle-aged—and the head honcho of Chalk Pharmaceuticals' Kansas City district.

Earlier that day, Beth had received news that her father had suffered a ministroke. Although he was safe and recovering in the hospital, she knew her presence would make all the difference.

Beth paused for a moment outside the restaurant and turned to her boss.

"Thanks again for allowing me to duck out a bit early, Chuck. I really appreciate it."

"Not a problem," Chuck said with a broad smile. "I'm just glad that you're able to make the first half of the meeting."

He opened the double doors for the lady and, after a quick wayward glance over his shoulder, followed her in.

The parking lot returned to stillness once more, the only movement being the shifting shadows as the moon made its way through the night sky. But then, the shadows in the back of the lot seemed to shake and grow until a dark figure emerged. Silently, the figure slipped beneath the lone Grand Prix.

It was only a few moments before a black Lincoln Town Car entered the parking lot and followed the same, unusual path that the Grand Prix had made earlier in the night. The car slowed as it neared Beth's car. Quickly, the passenger door opened and shut, and the car drove back into the night.

****

Beth clumsily dug through her purse to find her keys, lost among the dozens of business cards and cosmetics. The cold winter air made her fingers about as useful as garden trowels, and the glass of wine she'd had with dinner didn't help. Beth hadn't wanted to drink, not with her father in the hospital and a long drive ahead of her, but being the only woman in the district had certain pressures.

She knew facets of the business rather well. Her father had had a fantastic pharmaceutical sales career with a company headquartered in Kansas City, and he'd stressed to Beth how important these sales meetings are.

She found the keys and hurried into the car. Beth's thoughts turned to nothing but a big cup of hot coffee and the road ahead as she pulled out of the parking lot. After traveling a short distance, she stopped at a convenience store and purchased her jumbo cup of hot java.

She quickly returned to her car and began to traverse the steep, winding roads through the Ozark Hills. Unfortunately, she realized, it would be quite some time before she passed another sign of human life.

What she did not realize, but the moon did, was that the same car that the man jumped into after slipping under her vehicle was following her, keeping a quarter of a mile between them so as not to be seen.

Beth fumbled for her jumbo cup of caffeine and spilled it all over her lap. She unbuckled her seat belt and began cleaning up the spilled coffee with some Kleenex that she had in the console between the seats. After muttering a cussword or two for having stained her dress, she returned her focus to the winding road ahead of her, neglecting to re-buckle her seat belt.

Beth wished that she had taken a lid from the convenience store for the coffee, thinking that she could have avoided this fiasco. She also thought about calling her husband from her cell phone, but decided to wait until she was closer to Kansas City.

The woods she cut through were pitch-black, save for the snatches of tree and road illuminated by the Grand Prix's head-lights. Beth wished that she had the same views as she'd had during the drive down. Although the deep valleys were filled with bald trees and dead leaves, it had nevertheless been a beautiful vista. Besides, the darkness had a way of creeping up on her.

Beth was lost in her thoughts on what lived behind the wall of night, when she heard her phone ring. Beth let the call go to voicemail. If it was important, they would leave a message and she could return the call when she stopped for a new cup of coffee—with a lid. Hopefully, before she got all the way to Kansas City.

A moment later, the phone rang once more. Again, she let it go to voicemail, despite the sudden thoughts arising of her father in the hospital.

The phone rang a third time and this time, Beth opened her bag, scrambling frantically for the phone and trying to keep at bay the alarms going off in her head. This was no easy task; not only was Beth certain that her father had gone into some sort of cardiac arrest, but the more she felt around for the phone, the more it was pushed to the bottom.

Beth tried to keep her eyes on the road, blindly feeling for the phone and swerving as she glanced down to see into her bag. At last, she felt the hard plastic and snatched it out. She braced herself and looked at the caller ID.

Unknown caller? Maybe the hospital's unlisted?

Her sideways glance only lasted a split second, but when she looked back to the road, she had just enough time to pump the brakes in vain before crashing through the guardrail and soaring over the side of the cliff.

Minutes later, after the dust and rubble had settled on the obliterated Grand Prix, a pair of headlights rolled up and illuminated the now-jagged guardrail. The two men walked up to where Beth and her car had flown off the ridge. This time, both dark figures dressed in black appeared in the night while the full moon was out from behind the clouds, and they looked down into the ravine. They pulled out a bright halogen light, shined it down, and saw that Beth's car was upside down at the bottom of the snowy ravine.

The light from their halogen torch, coupled with the light emitted from the full moon, illuminated papers and pharmaceutical manuals that had been ejected from the car and which were now strewn all over the ravine. Without a seat belt to restrain her, Beth had also been thrown from the car, which had come to rest on top of her. The men could see her ankle and foot, with her yellow high-heeled shoe still on it, sticking out from under the vehicle.

The moon heard one of the men say, "The Grand Prix didn't catch fire and blow up, but there is no way anyone could have survived that car landing on top of them."

The moon realized that all this had taken only a few minutes and that no other vehicle had driven past in either lane of the road. There were no witnesses.

The two hurriedly jumped back into their car and the moon heard one of the men say, "We can definitely report back that the preemptive strike was a success!"

The moon looked down with great sadness on the horrendous site down below. How could these men have murdered this nice, professional young lady? What could cause them to commit such a heinous crime?

Though they say there is no water on the moon, the glowing orb shed many tears that night over southern Missouri before finally disappearing behind the clouds to grieve in solitude.

 # TWO

John O'Connor could not keep his mind on the road. He couldn't tell if it was the excitement of graduating from pharmacy school, or the fact that he'd landed his dream job with Chalk Pharmaceuticals, but he felt like he was on cloud nine. The last five years had flown by so fast, and now it was already the beginning of May 2003. And to top it off, he couldn't ask for a more beautiful day to be driving south on I-35 from Des Moines, Iowa, to Kansas City, Missouri.

John was born and raised in Kansas City and had always hoped for a good job offer to bring him back to the area where he grew up. His folks were elated when John told them he was coming back after graduating from the "Harvard of the Midwest," Des Moines' Drake University.

John was elated, too—but for different reasons. After receiving a top-notch education, he owed close to $100,000 in government and private loans. To a recent college graduate, that seems like an impossible burden to handle. But now that he had a job that came with a potential six-figure paycheck, John would be able to handle his debt and live comfortably too. His job at Chalk Pharma was like a dream come true!

As soon as he found out he had locked in the position, he drove down to Kansas City and picked out a duplex worthy of an up-and-coming pharmaceutical sales rep. He could not wait to furnish his new home with the type of furniture that the ladies would love.

It's not that he considered himself a playboy. On the contrary, John very much looked forward to domestic life and thought often of when and where he'd bump into his future bride. But for the time being, he was quite satisfied to sow a few wild oats with the model types he spotted at the restaurants and nightclubs on and near the Plaza, which was conveniently located next to his new abode.

John's best friend, Greg Clarke, was just a few years older and had already graduated from one of the local law schools. Now he worked as a young, upstart attorney, but had yet to start making the big bucks. He lived in a medium-sized apartment located just north of the Plaza. John could not wait to show off his new, upscale duplex to him. What a dichotomy between his future place and Greg's!

John kept feeling the need to pinch himself. Did he really land such a great job after five years of pharmacy school? After all, his best buddy attended *seven* years of post–high-school education—including three years of law school—and now he could only afford an average-sized apartment.

In some ways, it was hard for John to envision his friend as a lawyer. Growing up, Greg had been an iconoclast, always testing the patience of adults. But he wasn't all troublemaker; John knew there were many more sides to his friend, only revealed to those who got to know him.

John laughed out loud, thinking about his nickname in college. They called him *Milkman*. It never bothered John—he even kind of liked that nickname. After all, his favorite basketball player was Karl Malone, whose nickname, "The Mailman," was very similar.

John's nickname, of course, had nothing to do with his performance on the basketball court, even though he did look like a NBA basketball player, all six feet and five inches of him. The true reason why his frat brothers called John, "Milkman," was because his skin was as white as milk. *Better to be called a milkman rather than an albino,* he thought.

John glanced in his side-view mirror and realized that his blondish-red hair needed to be trimmed before he started training at his new job. He lowered his sunglasses to inspect his overall appearance. Again, he laughed out loud as he thought about another college memory. He had been dating a young coed on and off the last year of school when she told John, in a serious tone, that his eyes were an intoxicating blue "like the ocean near my parent's place in Norfolk, Virginia." Of course, John did not care what she thought of his eyes; he just wanted her to see his blue bedspread back in his frat room.

Finally, John entered the Kansas City metropolitan area just as the gas light flashed on his 1998, blue-with-white-trim T-top Trans Am and he realized it was time to stop daydreaming. As John filled *Bulldog,* his nickname for his car, he thought about the $10,000 he still owed on BD, but what the hell—John would be making big-ass bucks soon!

****

As John drove through Kansas City on I-35 and took Southwest Trafficway through the Plaza, he realized how much he had missed the sights and sounds of Kansas City in early summer. He was happy to pull into the driveway of his duplex, and happier still when he spotted a yellow 1988 Camaro parked on the block. He would know that car anywhere. Just as he threw BD into park, Greg jumped out of his car.

"You lucky son of a bitch! Not only do you have VD, but you snagged yourself a top-dog job!" Greg yelled.

"It's BD, not VD!" John shot back.

Greg smirked. He knew full well it was BD, after Drake's mascot, but the man had a proclivity for dirty jokes—one of his many charms.

John paused for a moment to take in Greg's appearance. His shirt was unbuttoned just enough to reveal his hairless chest; his pants, loose enough to hide his scrawny legs; and his baseball cap, strategically poised so as to disguise his receding hairline. But despite Greg's stature, his personality and boundless confidence made him seem like a bigger man.

"Check out the pad!" Greg exclaimed. "Great place to bring classy hens."

John led him to the front door and opened it to reveal his dream-come-true living room with stately white walls and built-in bookcases.

"Damn, Milkman, you'll blend right into the woodwork. You'd better get a mahogany bedroom set so the chicks will be able to find your white ass."

"Very funny," John replied.

****

Three hours and a case of Miller Genuine Draft later, John was relieved to see his friend speed away in his sputtering Camaro. Beat from the drive and the booze, John spread a sleeping bag on the empty living room floor and thought wistfully of his furniture that would arrive in the next couple of days.

Just as he was about to drift off to sleep, the phone rang. He had forgotten that his father had it activated the week before, so it gave him a start to hear the noise amidst the silence of his new home. He clumsily stood up, stumbled to the phone, and answered.

"Have you settled in?" an authoritative voice asked on the other end.

In his booze-induced daze, John realized it was none other than Chuck Frazier, his new boss. John struggled to find his voice.

"Mr. Frazier, how—how are you?"

"I'm fit as a fiddle, son," he responded.

John thought it was a strange response to come from a man who was making close to a couple hundred thousand or more a year. On the other hand, Chuck was the consummate salesman, and friendly colloquialisms such as this were a trait that John needed to learn quickly.

"Listen, I don't want to keep you," Chuck continued. "Lord knows you must be worn out from the drive down. Just wanted to check in and make sure you're finding Kansas City agreeable."

"Oh, I am, sir. Thank you, sir."

"Your company car will be available in the morning. We got you a brand-new Grand Prix. I hope it's to your liking, because if it's not, someone will be sorry!" Chuck paused to laugh.

11

He went on to say that his first shipment from Chalk Pharma headquarters in New Jersey was available for him to pick up at the UPS office nearest his duplex, and his office supplies were included in the shipment.

Just before signing off, his new boss requested his company at the Country Club Plaza for breakfast at 8 a.m. the day after tomorrow. John agreed, and the two said goodnight.

As soon as John hung up, a wave of nausea dizzied him. *Never again on a work night*, John thought, and stumbled back to his sleeping bag.

****

The next morning, John awoke to what sounded like a choir, but realized it was only the sound of his alarm clock filtered through his emotionally charged state of mind. He was ready to tackle the day. After he picked up his car, he would get a haircut, followed by some serious retail therapy on home goods. He was eager to start using his plastic on nice things.

During the cab ride over to the car dealership, John realized with a great deal of excitement that this was the first cab fee he could include on a company expense report! But he was even more blown away when he saw his sparkling new car waiting for him in the dealer lot.

After the day's tasks were complete, John headed back to his duplex and reflected on what lay ahead of him: his first day of training with Chalk Pharma, as well as breakfast with his new boss.

John relaxed and thought once more about how lucky he was to have a great job and be home, close to friends and family. He hadn't seen his parents yet, as they were on a two-week

Caribbean cruise. They certainly deserved it; John's dad had worked hard for thirty-five years for the same company and retired the previous year. They both led honest lives with decent jobs, but John knew that he didn't want to wait around until he was in his sixties to enjoy life. He wanted the good life now, and he was on track to get it!

Once more, John found himself drifting off in his sleeping bag when the phone rang. This time, it wasn't Mr. Frazier, but his buddy Greg.

"Oh man, you won't believe this leggy blond who's working for me now. I missed hitting the wastebasket every time just so I could see her bend over and pick it up for me. I wonder if the rug matches the drapes, if ya know what I mean—"

"Greg, I need to get some sleep," John interrupted and hung up. *Same old Greg.*

# THREE

John set out on his first trip in his primo company car. The new-car scent only fueled his excitement to start the job. He loved the black leather bucket seats and shiny wood paneling. He loved his new duplex. He loved his new life. And it was only the beginning. But first, he had to meet Mr. Frazier for breakfast.

On the way, he was treated to a gorgeous view of Brush Creek that sent his mind soaring back to junior high when he read about how mob boss Tom Pendergast paved it in the 1930s. Just across from the creek was the famous statue, *Married Love*, which portrayed Winston and Lady Churchill. John imagined a similar statue that he would place on his estate when he had his own country manor in Ireland, the home of his ancestors.

It only took a few minutes for John to drive from his duplex to the Fairmont Hotel. Upon entering the upscale coffee shop in the hotel, John was surprised to see Chuck Frazier already sitting at a table with coffee and a bagel, but not nearly as surprised as he was to see a gorgeous, blue-eyed, strawberry blonde woman sitting beside him. She looked a good twenty years younger than Mr. Frazier, and something about her reminded him of the actress Ann Margaret from the movies he'd watched as a kid.

As John approached the table, Mr. Frazier extended a stubby, puffy hand.

"Morning, John," he said. And then, turning to the woman beside him, "I'd like to introduce you to my wife, Ann."

John hoped that his face didn't betray the shock he was experiencing due to the fact that not only was this woman's name Ann, but that she was also Chuck's wife. He shook hands with her, noticing that her skin was as creamy and fair as his own.

"Well, I think this is my cue, boys," she said as she stood up. She turned and kissed her husband before shyly bidding them both good-bye and leaving the coffee shop.

If he wasn't before, John was now positive that he had chosen the right job. Here was Mr. Frazier, a middle-aged, balding, overweight man who nevertheless had it all. Granted, he had a charm about him, but John was sure it was the job that got him everything he wanted—and more.

Chuck seemed to be reading his mind as he said, "John, I am a lucky old fart."

"Yes, sir," John replied.

"Did you see the rock on her hand?" he asked.

Of course John hadn't. He was too busy noticing her other interesting assets.

"That rock cost me fifty-six grand!" Chuck continued. "Picked it out herself. I'd been married before, but it was her first so I said go ahead. You know the moral of that story, John?"

"What's that?"

"Always remember, it's only money!" he cackled.

John laughed and glanced out the window in time to see Ann get into a white Bimmer and drive off. Mr. Frazier watched as his gaze lingered.

"Like that car, for instance," he continued. "I was brought up the old-fashioned way. I bought that little car for her strictly on a cash-and-carry basis. That's the best way to do business, wouldn't you agree?"

John's thoughts were drifting down the street in a little white BMW, so it took him a moment to realize his boss was speaking to him.

"Yes. Absolutely," he stammered. He immediately regretted this display of thoughtlessness. His boss may have been portly and jovial, but there was definitely something about him that was downright intimidating. First-day jitters, John figured.

"Very good," said Mr. Frazier. He reached into his coat pocket, pulled out a ticket, and put it on the table. It was a round-trip ticket to New Jersey set for the beginning of the following week.

"We're sending you out to HQ for our standard, two-week training period for Chalk Pharmaceutical." He then reached into his coat pocket again, but this time retrieved a folded wad of cash.

"I want you to have fun while you're out there," he said, counting out a row of twenties. "But I also want you to concentrate on passing those exams. Don't worry about sales training techniques. Chuck Frazier, the ol' detail-man himself, will teach you how to sell."

John's eyes lit up, although he felt slightly uneasy being handed a large amount of cash directly out of his boss's pocket. "Thanks, sir. This is awful generous of you."

"It's not company standard, but think nothing of it." He placed the money roll back in his pocket. "Until the trip, just focus on settling in. Unpack your office, relax, maybe meet a nice girl. Do whatever so you're ready for next week."

John blushed, unused to speaking so candidly with a man of such power.

"Hey—," his boss went on, "I've got all the confidence in the world in you. Don't worry a thing about training. After all, you already made it through one of the best pharmacy schools in the country." He stopped speaking and looked up as a waitress approached their table.

"Can I take your order?" she asked.

Mr. Frazier gestured for John to begin.

"Well, I—"

John stopped mid-sentence after glancing up from his menu. Before him stood the most drop-dead gorgeous waitress he had ever seen. Cute and petite, she was absolutely stunning with large, almond-shaped brown eyes and an olive complexion.

"Yes?" she encouraged.

"Uh, a bagel and hot chocolate," he stuttered, and then handed her his utensil roll.

When she realized his mistake, she laughed, and instead gently lifted the menu from his hand.

His boss watched intently as she walked off.

"Yeah, Sara's a real doll. Works full-time at St. Luke's Hospital too. Busy girl, but always with a smile."

Two gorgeous women before nine o'clock in the morning—this wasn't what John had remembered from high school, but he wasn't in high school anymore.

****

After John's hot chocolate came, he sipped sparingly, making the soothing, warm drink last as long as possible so he could watch Sara as she worked her tables.

"Can I ask you a question, Mr. Frazier?"

"What can I do for you, son?"

Chuck's reply was quick and direct, which, as John was learning, was how he spoke. Most people would equate his mannerisms to arrogance, but John didn't think so. He believed that the way his boss communicated had an effect on people that secured their loyalty to him with unquestioning obedience. The man was authoritative.

"How did Chalk Pharmaceutical acquire its name?" John asked.

"Well, you just might find that story interesting, seeing as you grew up in the Kansas City area." Chuck took a gulp of steaming coffee before continuing. "The founder of the company went to KU many decades ago when Wilt Chamberlain played basketball for the Jayhawks. As you probably know, or at least I hope you'd know, the Jayhawks' chant is 'ROCK CHALK, JAYHAWK!'" He pumped his fist in the air as he repeated the battle cry.

He explained how the basketball arena was divided into three sections. Each section chanted one of the words in progression, like the wave. His section had to yell 'CHALK' as loud as they could, at just the right moment. He demonstrated as he told the story, and a few of the café's patrons glanced over their shoulders as Chuck yelled out again.

"And that's where Chalk Pharmaceutical comes from," he said. "Simple as that. And it turned out to be a good choice! I'd say our company's just as successful—if not more—than KU's basketball program."

John couldn't help but laugh at the irony of such an important company being named after such a simple story.

"All right, now do me a favor and get the hell out of here," he said cheerfully, slapping John on the shoulder. "I'll call you every now and then while you're out in Jersey to see how things are going. And remember to have some fun, will ya?"

John heartily agreed and rose from the table. As he made his way to the door, his boss shouted, "Hey! I forgot to tell ya, one of the Chalk Pharma reps will be calling you today or tomorrow. Name is Ryan Starr. No coincidence he's our star rep! You'll wanna watch what he does!"

What an interesting play on words, John mused.

He turned and started again toward the door, but stopped when he spotted Sara. Scrambling to think of something to say to her, he asked, "Do you know where I might find a pay phone?"

"Yes, John. Just outside in the foyer."

Hearing her say his name made his heart skip a beat, and it also gave him a glimmer of hope that she might be interested in him especially since she acknowledged him by his name. He decided to use the phone first before asking her out.

As soon as John got to the phone, he realized that he had no reason to use it. But keeping up the act, he picked up the phone and called the first person he could think of.

"Office of Greg Clarke," an airy, feminine voice answered on the other end.

"Yes, can you transfer me? This is Dr. Smith calling about those lab test results. I'm afraid I have some bad news."

"Oh, yes. Please hold," she replied, flustered, and put him on hold.

It was a few moments before Greg picked up.

"John, you bastard!" he yelled.

"How's it going, old buddy?" John asked.

"You just ruined my chances with Ms. Legs; that's how it's going."

"Well, tell ya what: Maybe we can find something else at lunch. Meet me at Houston's at noon?"

"Yeah, fine. Merry Christmas and a happy screw you!"

John hung up the phone and reentered the coffee shop. He glanced around to find Sara, and was surprised to see that a new guest had joined his boss at the table. Chuck was sitting with his back to John and didn't see that he was still in the restaurant, so John was free to give this new guy the once-over.

The man sitting opposite from Chuck was elderly, but his outdated suit and dress hat made him seem even more ancient, as if he were transported straight from the sixties. It may have been due to old age, but there was something about the way his mouth sneered to the side that gave him a sinister look.

Suddenly, John felt uncomfortable, as if he were spying on his boss with this man. After all, it was none of his business whom his boss met with, so he didn't think a thing more of it after spotting Sara coming back from the kitchen.

Borrowing a note from his old friend, John strolled over to Sara with unbridled confidence. He decided to be straightforward, just like Mr. Frazier was in dealing with people. And it worked: Sara smiled back at him.

"So, I was thinking . . . what do you think about catching a movie sometime this week? Or maybe dinner? Both?"

He waited to hear her excuse—stage one of the typical female's dating game—but was instead surprised by her reply.

"Actually, how would you like to be my escort? There's this Filipino Association dinner on Friday night. It's nothing too fancy, but it would be nice to have some company. What do you think?"

John quickly agreed and Sara wrote down her contact information. He glanced at the slip of paper before tucking it into his shirt pocket. At the top, it read "Sara Williamson."

"That's interesting," he said.

"What's that?"

"Well, for someone going to the Filipino Association dinner, you certainly have a very old-school Northern Irish last name."

For the first time, an unpleasant look clouded her face and he immediately regretted his observation.

"Williamson is from my ex-husband. He was American." She glanced hastily around the restaurant. "Look, when I see you on Friday, I'll tell you more about myself, OK?" After she said this, a smile returned to her face.

At that moment, a deep, raspy voice called out Sara's name. They both looked and John saw that it was the man with Mr. Frazier, motioning with a coffee cup in hand.

Sara rolled her eyes.

"I hate waiting on that old guy. I don't care if he tips better than anyone else here. He just gives me the creeps. And the gangster rumors don't help his cause."

John couldn't help but laugh. How could this feeble, old man be involved in illicit affairs?

"It's not funny," Sara snapped. "I hear people call him *Simple Simon*." She lowered her voice as she said his name. "Anyway, gotta run. Call me!"

John watched her walk toward his boss's booth, and then decided to hightail it out of the restaurant before he was noticed. He was certain that Sara had been mistaken about the old man, but still, he couldn't help but wonder why his boss was having coffee with someone with such a reputation, true or false.

 # FOUR

Although he was miles away from the coffee shop, John's thoughts were still back with his boss and the suspicious character with whom he was meeting. He simply couldn't shake the idea that Chuck Frazier was meeting with a gangster. As he made his way to pick up his company cell phone, he thought of possible explanations.

That's when it hit him: Mr. Frazier was very involved with his church. In fact, he taught Sunday school every weekend. The man who he saw in the coffee shop was probably someone he knew from church. The thought of this eased his mind, at least for the time being.

By the time John arrived at Houston's for lunch with Greg, he had all but forgotten the Simple Simon matter. Instead, his thoughts had turned to more serious matters, like getting to know Sara on their first date, Friday night. He imagined what she would look like dolled up for a night out on the town. And then, of course, his mind naturally progressed to later on in the night . . . a bottle of wine . . . low lights . . . soft music . . .

"Hey buddy, over here!" Greg interrupted his trance and called him over to the bar.

****

As they ate lunch—cheeseburgers and fries, a Midwest classic—John remembered just why Greg had been his lifelong friend. While he usually showed off his fun, wild side to friends and strangers, with John, Greg also allowed his intellectual, articulate characteristics to come out. The two trusted each other completely and were able to just be themselves around each other.

"Have you ever heard of a guy named Simple Simon?" John asked.

He fully expected his friend to roar with laughter after hearing such a ridiculous name for someone who was supposedly a gangster, but instead, Greg's face turned to stone.

"What about that low-life criminal?" he demanded.

John explained how he had come across the man with his boss.

Once he was finished recounting the experience, Greg asked, "Remember that summer I spent interning at the United States District Attorney's Office downtown? Well, Simple Simon was practically a household name, except no one wanted to say it."

"What do you mean?" John asked.

"I mean that Simple Simon is not only *in* the mafia, but at the top of the food chain when it comes to the Kansas City mob circuit."

"No way. Then what was he doing with my boss?"

Greg gulped the rest of his Coke and gestured to the waitress for a refill.

"Are you sure this guy was Simple Simon?"

"Well," John replied, "I have no idea. Sara was the one who pointed him out."

"Who the hell is Sara?" Greg asked.

John spoke up quickly, "Sara's this knockout waitress I met this morning. And I don't know why she would know anything about the mob. You know, the more I think about it, the more I'm certain that it was probably a member of Mr. Frazier's church."

"Huh. Sounds like Sara is your typical woman. Always gossiping, always sticking her nose where it doesn't belong."

John rolled his eyes. *Typical, chauvinist Greg speaking.* He decided to change the subject.

"So where do these mafia people come from?"

Greg rolled up his sleeves as if he were about to embark on a lengthy summation to the jury.

"Simple Simon's group is connected to the traditional mafia from Sicily. According to some of the law enforcement officers who would come through the DA's office, most of them live over by the Kansas City Museum, right across from where the JFK Memorial was dedicated by the American Legion."

John was surprised to realize that he had forgotten where the JFK Memorial was located. Both he and Greg were big fans of the late president. John was even named after him. Greg suggested that they take a trip there to check it out. He thought it would be fun to also go to the Museum, especially since they hadn't been since they were kids on a field trip.

****

Before departing, Greg shook John's hand and, assuming his best attorney voice, told him, "Forget about this shit with your boss and whomever he was talking to. Sara sounds like a nice girl, but I'm sure she doesn't know anything concerning the underworld, here or anywhere else."

"You're probably right," John agreed.

The two began to climb into their respective cars when Greg called out, "Hey! You should be worrying about her sexy underwear. Not whether she's knows someone in the KC mob, am I right?"

John nodded and climbed into his car. He turned his thoughts toward the work ahead of him and started back home to begin studying for the upcoming two-week training session.

****

John arrived home and noticed the blinking light on his answering machine, announcing the calls he had missed while he was out. He hit the play button and listened to a beep, immediately followed by a gruff, fast-speaking male voice:

"Hey, John. Ryan Starr here. Meet me at Classic Cup at five thirty. On the Plaza. Me and my associate, Joe Arnold, will be waiting."

At the end of the message, John heard another chime, this one coming from the front door. It was the deliverymen with his new furniture set. They brought each piece in and left only after John signed the delivery receipt. John briefly thought about the price tag for it all—a little over $25,000 charged to his credit card. A small price to pay for good taste, but even more invaluable was the fact that John would not have to sleep on the floor again.

After he arranged the furniture, he unpacked the boxes he had picked up earlier, containing Chalk Pharma office supplies.

He opened the laptop they sent separately and brought up the instructions for the modules he needed to study before going to Jersey. The instructions indicated that he would be tested on materials included under the Prescription Drug Marketing Act of 1987 on his first day of training at HQ. The last module in his training material went into complete detail about the PDMA for his preparation. All this information pertained to the all-important samples that he would receive from, and distribute to, physicians on behalf of Chalk Pharma when he returned from training.

After finishing four of the twelve modules, John decided to test out his new mahogany bed before meeting Ryan and Joe at the Classic Cup. A nap would have been nice, but he mostly tossed and turned, thinking about Greg's remark concerning Sara's underwear. Did she wear bikini panties? Or a thong? At this rate, he would never get to sleep.

John's attraction to Sara was more than just physical. There was something about her that took his breath away and made his heart beat just a little bit faster. Though he was scared to admit it, he had never felt this way about any woman.

The alarm went off at five o'clock and he got up and left for the Classic Cup. On his drive over, he wondered what Ryan Starr and Joe Arnold would be like. One thing he knew for sure: If they worked for Chuck Frazier, then they were damn-good pharmaceutical reps!

 # FIVE

It wasn't until after John had entered the Classic Cup that he realized he had no way of knowing who either of his two coworkers would be. He was spared from wandering around aimlessly when a man who appeared to be in his late twenties approached him at the bar.

"John O'Connor?"

"How did you know?" John asked.

The man held up a yellow manila folder and opened it, revealing a stack of papers with John's picture on top.

"Company records," he replied. "Ryan Starr." The man held out his hand.

John shook it, surprised that he was allowed to look at employee records. It only confirmed his suspicion that Ryan was Chuck's right-hand man, maybe even his prodigy. Of course, now that he had joined the company, that role might soon be taken over . . .

The closer he looked at Ryan, the more he noticed the similarities between the two men. Ryan was about five foot eight with a stocky build and a virtual copy including Mr. Frazier's stubby, puffy hands. The only difference was that Ryan had a full head of brown hair, and did not wear glasses. This guy could have been Mr. Frazier's clone, only thirty years younger.

"So where's Joe?" John asked.

"He should be arriving any minute. In the meantime, how about we grab a table on the patio?"

They moved to an outdoor table and ordered a round of beers. Ryan also ordered two cognacs.

"Uh, I hate to say it, but I'm saving my cash to take to Jersey—," John began before Ryan cut him off.

"Don't worry about the booze. Chuck'll pick up the tab," he said and laughed decadently.

This keeps getting better! John thought.

Joe Arnold arrived after their third beer and second cognac. There was a monumental difference between Ryan and Joe. While Ryan dressed stylishly and was immaculately groomed, Joe, a good six inches taller and with the physique of a former NFL linebacker, appeared shabby. His suit looked about two sizes too small, and his tie hung loose around his collar. His eyes were tired and searching, as if he were walking around without his glasses. Joe looked to be about the same age as Mr. Frazier—late fifties, if he had to guess.

Joe took a seat and they ordered another round of drinks. Joe volunteered to drink John's next round of booze.

"So, down to business, right?" Ryan began.

"I suppose," Joe followed, "you're probably wondering what it's like to work for Mr. Frazier. All you need to remember is that

Chuck operates on the honor system. He's got your back so long as you never betray him. Keep on Chuck's good side, and you'll have the best boss in the world!"

"That's right, buddy," said Ryan. "Don't do anything to piss off Chuck. He is a man who believes in more than just getting even."

"Don't fuck with Chuck," Joe agreed.

John thought his coworkers' aggressive approach was an attempt to give him—the new guy—a shakedown. But he listened attentively anyway.

"This district is not a democracy, but a monarchy. And Chuck is the king. Treachery will not be allowed," Ryan warned.

"Yeah, and treason is a hanging offense," Joe muttered as he sipped on his beer. As he did this, John noticed that his left hand was covered in bandages.

"What, have you been using Ginsu knives lately?" John joked.

Joe glanced at his hand and muttered, "Nah, it's from last night's shucking party."

Ryan sputtered, choking on his drink. "Man!" he coughed, "I think we need to stop drinking for the night."

"What the hell is a shucking party?" John asked.

Joe hastily replied, "What? Shucking party? No, I said the *sucking party*. I went to a party last night that sucked."

Ryan's eyes shot daggers at him as he stumbled on.

"And I cut my fingers while cutting fruit for my wife to take to this . . . party . . . that really . . . sucked."

It took John a few moments to comprehend this new information. The rounds of drinks had gone to his head after all, and it made it difficult for John to understand exactly what was going on. So instead, he simply shrugged it off and announced that it was time for him to head back.

Ryan quickly stood up to say good-bye, while Joe remained seated, downing the rest of his beer with John's untouched beer in his other hand. Even though Ryan expressed disappointment that John was leaving so early, his face appeared quite relieved. John tucked this image away for future analysis.

****

Once home, John galloped from the front door and dove on top of his brand-new bed, still rumpled from the nap he took a few hours earlier. The alarm clock on his bedroom dresser read 9:30 p.m. It was one of his many new toys, thanks to his shiny new piece of plastic. The clock cost him $500, and in addition to its sleek design, it had an array of features, such as a programmable voice that called out the time every half hour.

John figured it was still early enough to see if Sara was at home. He dialed her number and was surprised when she picked it up after the first ring.

"John, hi! I'm so glad you called," she said.

"You are?"

"Yeah, but unfortunately, I have some bad news. As it turns out, I have to work Friday night. I thought I had the night off from St. Luke's, but one of the nurses came down with a kidney infection so they're going to need me. I won't be able to go to the Filipino Association dinner after all."

John had the unfortunate habit of laughing at inappropriate occasions after he had been drinking. Tonight was no exception. As soon as he heard the bit about the kidney infection, he couldn't help but snicker.

"John, have you been drinking?"

John froze, not knowing how to answer. So instead, he just said that he had spent the evening at the Classic Cup with his two new coworkers. He braced himself for her response.

"Well, in that case, how about I grab a bottle of white wine and we make it a party? You can show me your place."

Stunned, John quickly agreed, and then jumped off his bed to tidy his duplex for her arrival.

****

Fifteen minutes passed between their phone call and the doorbell ringing, which was music to John's ears. She smiled and presented him with a bottle of German Riesling wine and a Tupperware dish.

"Don't tell me you cooked," John began.

"Oh, just a little midnight snack for us to munch on."

Before he could stop himself, John blurted out, "I think *you're* the midnight snack." He immediately regretted the remark, but to his surprise, she was very relaxed and her smile broadened.

She opened the container and said, "Fried peanuts with garlic—a traditional Filipino dish."

"Looks like someone doesn't want to get too close tonight," John commented.

Sara pulled out her small, red patent-leather purse and retrieved a tin of mints.

"I'm two steps ahead of you, junior."

"I think we're going to get along just fine," John replied, and led her inside.

Sara followed behind.

"Well, judging by your décor and the fact that you can't keep your eyes off of my shorts, I think I'd have to agree." Her eyes twinkled deviously.

It was true—Sara had on a pair of pink hot pants to match her pink midriff tank top and it was driving him absolutely wild. But even in his semi-drunken state, he knew that Sara was a quality lady, and things weren't going to go very far.

"So, where do you keep the wine glasses?" she asked.

He held up a bag of red, plastic cups and cheekily grinned.

"You've got to be kidding me! John, my first gift to you will be a set of wine glasses. Or should I say, *big-boy glasses*."

"At least I have a wine opener," he protested. What he left out was that he had saved it from his college days when it was used solely for its bottle-cap–removing capabilities. But she didn't need to know that.

Sara opened the bottle, poured them each a glass, and they settled into John's new couch to enjoy the wine. At first, she had a lot of questions for John. Where did he go to school? Why did he decide to go into pharmaceutical sales? But then, halfway through the fried peanuts and bottle of wine, John turned the topic of conversation to her, so that she would talk about herself.

She told him that she had been raised in Manila, and her father worked in Makati, which was the "Manhattan" of Manila. Her father had sold stocks in companies that didn't have ADRs listed on the New York Stock Exchange and made a very successful living for himself.

John noticed that both of their wine glasses were empty, and was just about to ask if she wanted a beer when the clock in his bedroom announced "twelve midnight."

"Probably time to call it a night, huh?" she asked John.

"You got far to go?"

"St. Luke's. I live in a townhouse by the hospital to make it easy on myself. It's only a short ride."

"Do you own your townhouse?" he asked, then stopped and said, "Sorry, that was nosy of me."

"Not at all," she laughed. "Actually, my parents passed away back in '96 and I inherited the townhouse from them debt-free. I guess I should also mention that I have a brother and two sisters who share my parents' mansion and estate back in Manila. That's where they live. But I'm the baby, so I had to seek my adventure in the States."

John couldn't help but stare at her. The more he learned, the more he fell for her.

"Finished with the interrogation, or can I expect to be hand-cuffed?" she teased.

"Stick around any longer, and I just might hold you to that."

She turned to head out. Suddenly, John remembered that he would be heading out soon. He told her about the training program he would complete in New Jersey over the next two weeks. She seemed genuinely saddened to hear the news, so he decided that now was not the appropriate time to tell her the other part of the story: that in another two to three months, he would be going to Chicago for an additional two-week training session at the regional office, followed by yet another session two to three months after that. *Best to tackle one thing at a time,* he thought.

Before she left, he promised to call her from New Jersey. There was an awkward moment where they weren't sure how to say good-bye, but almost on cue, they moved in sync and before he knew what had happened, they were embracing in a kiss that would carry him through the next two weeks and beyond.

 # SIX

If Chuck had treated John like a king in Kansas City, Chalk Pharma doubled their efforts in New Jersey. Not only was he put up in a luxurious hotel, but also, all of his meals were taken care of and his generous per diem included spending money for his own devices.

They ate at the best restaurants in Manhattan. John even tried Wagyu beef for the first time. Up until then, John had believed that there wasn't any kind of beef besides the stuff that came out of the good-old Midwest. Never had it felt so right to be wrong. Wagyu beef was called the caviar of beef, and its smooth flavor, like a fine liqueur, lived up to expectation.

He followed it up with some of the finest tobacco money could buy—a Davidoff cigar. As an Irish-Catholic boy, John had always looked up to the Kennedys for his style and taste. While perusing the tobacco shop, he remembered reading that JFK smoked fine cigars, which is why he purchased the cigars.

It wasn't all play, however; there was, after all, work to be done. But Chuck was right—after making it through Drake, none of it was too difficult. He flew through the Pharmacology for the pharmaceuticals both he, and his competitors, would be selling.

The most intriguing material that he had studied at home, and had now heard a lecture about and was tested on, were the guidelines for handling, storing, and distributing prescription drug samples. While he was in pharmacy school, John had no idea how strict the laws were regarding pharmaceutical samples. The biggest concern was people illegally diverting samples into the gray market.

The Federal Food and Cosmetic Act authorized investigators to inspect any place where samples were held and carried, without a warrant. John saw this as an infringement on a salesperson's constitutional rights. The loophole around this was that the inspection was limited to places where samples are *traditionally* stored or held. If the FDA investigator wanted to search other areas, then he had to have a warrant or subpoena in order to do so.

Chalk Pharma advised that if this ever happened to one of the representatives, he or she was to ask the investigator to telephone the corporation's general counsel before consenting to the search. The legal consequences of noncompliance with the PDMA were very severe. The PDMA imposes several criminal penalties if one fails to comply with the requirements of the law. For instance, if a person sells, purchases, or trades a drug sample, then they are subject to imprisonment for no more than ten years, or there could be an additional fine of no more than $250,000. Or both of these actions could be enforced.

John found it interesting that Chalk Pharma was liable if one of their reps was convicted of wrongdoing. That involved a civil penalty of no more than $50,000 for each of the first two violations resulting in a conviction of a rep in any ten-year period. Second, there was a civil penalty of no more than one million dollars after a second conviction of any rep in any ten-year period. Finally, a civil penalty could be assessed against Chalk Pharma for no more than $100,000 for failing to report the conviction of one of its reps for illegal activity involving samples to the government.

Chalk Pharma had a retired FBI agent on staff to investigate any alleged illegal activity. If any of the reps were approached by someone encouraging them to perform any illegal acts concerning his or her samples, then he or she was to contact the company's FBI agent and it would be handled confidentially and discreetly.

If anything, Chalk Pharma was skilled at handling matters confidentially and discreetly. John only realized how true this was when he learned the unsettling background to how his position had opened up, enabling him to get the job.

During one of their nights on the town wining and dining, one of his trainers let it slip that the sales rep before him had been a young woman by the name of Beth Beacon. She had been at her district company meeting in Lake of the Ozarks, and as Beth was driving home, she lost control and went off a cliff.

John had visited the Ozarks many times, and knew how winding and treacherous those roads through the bluffs could be. But still, it gave him an eerie feeling to know that he'd replaced somebody who had died in the line of duty.

****

"We ask that all passengers please put their seat and tray in the upright position, and power down all electrical devices as we begin our descent into Kansas City," the flight attendant directed over the intercom.

After two, long weeks in New Jersey, John had spent the flight home dozing and was ready for more as soon as he got home to his duplex and plush, king-sized bed.

His weariness melted away as soon as he set eyes on Sara. John had told her that he would take a cab home from the airport, but she refused. Now he was glad that she had. There was no better sight than a beautiful woman waving and jumping up and down with excitement upon her loved one's return.

She ran up to John, threw her arms around his neck, and gave him a firm, welcome-home kiss. As they embraced, Sara whispered in John's ear, "Maybe tonight we can do better than kissing."

"In that case, why are we still standing here?" John quipped. Sara giggled with delight and ran ahead to start the car.

It was difficult to imagine anyone treating someone like Sara poorly. She was kind, beautiful, intelligent. Her ex-husband hadn't appreciated any of that, as Sara had told him during one of their long phone calls while he was in Jersey. She had caught him in bed with another woman and "dumped him like a bag of shit," as she'd put it. *Good riddance*, John thought.

Sara pulled around in her black 1999 Jeep Cherokee. As John dropped his bags in back, he noticed there were already a few wrapped parcels on the seat.

"Are all those presents for me, or did you meet someone new while I was gone?" he joked.

Laughing, Sara responded, "Well aren't you a funny one? Actually, three of these gifts are for you, one is for me, and one is for us."

"Onward, captain!" John cried. Home couldn't get there fast enough.

****

As they got closer to John's duplex, Sara suggested they instead go to her townhouse to open the gifts and talk. John thought it was a great idea—especially since it was closer.

Once they reached her townhouse, she pulled out two of the packages and told John to leave the rest and follow her up to her place. After a brief walk up the driveway, he stepped inside and took in the low lighting and thick, shag carpets of Sara's home. It was the perfect bungalow for a girl like Sara.

She gave John one of the packages.

"Open it and wait here. I'll be right back." She ran off down the hallway with the other package in hand.

John ripped open the package to reveal a bottle of wine. He looked closer, and realized that it was the same vintner of wine they had drunk the night before he left. John started to look around the kitchen for an opener when Sara called to him.

"John, will you come here for a minute?"

She did not have to ask twice. John almost tripped over his feet while speeding down the hall. Wafts of perfume drew him into her bedroom where she was waiting for him in a white negligee and bright-red panties. In one hand, she had two wine glasses, and in the other, a corkscrew. Two steps ahead of him, indeed! This was one homecoming he would never forget.

****

John finally got back to his duplex at seven thirty the next morning when Sara dropped him off before work. As he turned the lock on the door, he heard the phone ringing and sprinted to answer it.

"Where the fuck have you been, Milkman?" Greg asked. "I tried reaching you until one o'clock last night."

"Actually, I just walked in the door," he responded.

"Oh, I get it; you pick a hot Filipino over your best friend," he said.

"Greg, you know I don't kiss and tell, but your educated guess is right."

Greg was happy to know that his friend had met a nice girl. More importantly, he wanted to know if they could get together for drinks at six. John told him that he would have to call back after he settled in. At the moment, he was just too exhausted.

After they hung up, John listened to the stream of messages that had been left in his absence. The last message was from Ryan Starr. His message was simply, *"Meet me at the Fairmont on the Plaza for lunch at noon."*

 # SEVEN

John arrived at the Fairmont at twelve, sharp. He knew that Sara would not be in, since she was working at the hospital that day. As he entered the coffee shop, he saw Chuck Frazier's hand go up and wave him over. Ryan Starr and Joe Arnold were seated next to him, along with a few unfamiliar faces.

"Hi. I'm Mike Currey," a man who looked to be in his late thirties introduced himself to John as he sat down.

Another hand stuck out in front of him.

"And I'm Mavis Turner. Nice to meet you."

After all the introductions had been made, John joked, "So I take it this is an all-male club?"

"It is now," Ryan said. John grimaced and thought of Beth Beacon, but decided now was not the time to bring up that story.

"Well, John, that's not entirely true," came a female voice from behind his shoulder.

He turned around and saw that it was Mrs. Frazier, who was working her way to a chair near her husband.

As she sat down, he noticed what a nice figure she had, which reminded him of the figure he'd had the night before.

Mrs. Frazier must have noticed a smile on his face because she remarked, "John, the East Coast must have agreed with you. You seem to be in a happy mood."

"Yes, I had a great time in Jersey," he replied.

"Now you're entering the real phase of your training," Chuck interrupted. "It's called The Chuck Frazier School of Experience."

The table erupted in laughter.

"You'll be working with Ryan out in the field part of this week," he continued.

John nodded at Ryan, who seemed to be wearing a smile as well, or more appropriately—a shit-eating grin.

John looked around the table and sized up the team. By the looks his colleagues wore, he knew that Mr. Frazier's people really did respect him. He looked at Mike, and noticed that he had a conciliatory manner about him, as though he was wary of stepping on anyone's toes.

Mavis, on the other hand, seemed to have a unique talent. Mavis could crystallize his opinion on a subject, and then later say the exact opposite, and nobody would notice. Or maybe it was just that no one cared.

"As you all know," began Mr. Frazier, "we have a new competitor. Faxlot is a new, nonsteroidal anti-inflammatory drug that could cause huge problems for us. Therefore, I want all of you to report to me at the minimum of once per week. Tell me all activities that you see in promotion of this product.

"There are going to be quite a few stock sample bottles to launch this product. Keep an eye on our heavy prescribers of nonsteroidals in our territories."

"We'll take care of those stock bottles," Joe murmured.

Ryan, Mavis, and Chuck laughed, but John noticed that Mike looked confused, as did Mrs. Frazier. John was certain he had the same look.

After discussing the features and benefits of Faxlot, the group ordered lunch. Mrs. Frazier ordered a salad with oil and vinegar, which looked comical next to her husband's patty melt and French fries. Everything about this couple seemed mismatched.

As the group finished up lunch, Chuck interjected on John's behalf and spoke of his reasons for hiring him.

Besides the obvious—his education, extracurriculars, and personality—he explained, "The reason I hired John was because he would make a good power forward on the district basketball team at Regionals and when we play pick-up games at the district meetings!"

Everybody laughed, but he wondered why Chuck didn't say anything about Mavis. When he stood up, the man must have been at least six foot eight.

The group started to head out. As if on cue, Mrs. Frazier kissed her husband and said good-bye to the remaining employees.

Before John left the coffee shop, Ryan called out for him. He walked back to see what he wanted.

"I'll pick you up tomorrow. Eight thirty a.m. I already have your address," Ryan said.

John confirmed and was about to head out again, when Mr. Frazier asked if he would stick around to meet his friend,

Simon. John hadn't realized that anyone else had joined them, but there he was—the same old man from that morning when he first met Sara.

As John shook Simon's hand, he noticed that his eyes were as cold as steel. His hand was practically icy and clammy, and shook slightly. Standing at his side was a tall, muscular black woman in her thirties.

"This is my nurse, Belle," Simon introduced.

She stepped forward to shake hands with John, and he noticed that her hand enveloped his like a baseball glove.

"Mr. Simon is my investment partner in a retirement home nearby," Chuck explained.

"Pleasure to meet you," John replied.

"You have a good day tomorrow with Ryan. I'll give you a call at the end of the week," Chuck said. John took this as his cue to exit.

He decided to use the restroom first. On the way in, he couldn't help but think of how strange the three of them looked as they sat back down at the table. Belle gave John the creeps, not to mention, Simon just seemed mean.

As he entered the bathroom, he ran into Mike and Mavis drying their hands. They didn't see him, and so he caught the last part of their conversation.

"What did Ryan mean about taking care of those stock bottles?" Mike asked.

Mavis had a mean look on his face, but when he saw John, it softened.

"Don't worry about things you don't understand," he said. "Just take care of your Topeka territory. Now let's get out of here."

The two left with nothing more than a glance at John.

****

John arrived back at his duplex and was about to relax on his couch, when he remembered the other packages that Sara had given him. He grabbed them from the kitchen table and opened them, one at a time.

The first package contained a set of four wine glasses—just as Sara had promised. The second package consisted of a small, brown jug labeled "Straight Corn Whiskey." It was distilled and bottled by a company in Weston, Missouri, which was just northwest of Kansas City. Along with the whiskey came a note:

"This is to help you get through the lonely nights when I have to work."

The third package held a gift pack of Japanese sake, and four sake cups with a bottle to heat the liquid. This one also had a personal note:

"Save the sake to drink with me so I can tell if you like it!"

He smiled at Sara's thoughtfulness, and then looked at the clock and realized it was almost time to meet Greg for drinks. Before heading out, he decided to leave Chuck a message to tell him how grateful he was for the chance to prove that he could do a good job for Chalk Pharma. Not only was it good manners, but it was also heartfelt.

Then he realized that he hadn't confirmed with Greg, so he dialed him next. The receptionist answered and transferred him, and John wondered if it was the same long-legged dream girl who had been there before, or if Greg had scared her off already.

"Hello, Mr. O'Connor," Greg answered. Judging by the formality, John knew right away that there must have been a client in the office with him, so he decided to have some fun at Greg's expense.

"Hey, barrister, is there a long-legged hen under that desk?"

"N-no, Mr. O'Connor," Greg stuttered.

"Well, how about this, let's meet at six o'clock and get you a nice head—on your beer, that is."

"Yes, Mr. O'Connor, where would you like to meet?"

"Classic Cup. I'll be outside on the patio. Invite that long-legged hen too, if you want."

"She no longer works here," Greg muttered.

Before hanging up, John yelled, "So much for the head!"

****

John arrived early at the Classic Cup and noticed a familiar white BMW parked outside. He went inside and saw that Mrs. Frazier was sitting alone on the patio. She motioned him over.

"What are you doing here?" she asked.

"I was about to ask you the same question."

"Chuck is having a men's church meeting tonight, so I decided to treat myself to drinks and dinner out."

John looked down and saw that she was enjoying a fancy salmon dish with a glass of white wine.

He was about to mention how much he admired her car, but before he could, he heard a familiar voice behind him: "Who is this beautiful blonde?"

"Here comes trouble," John said to himself.

Mrs. Frazier extended her hand to Greg.

"Thank you for the compliment," she said.

John jumped in and made introductions. Greg not only shook her hand, but kissed her cheek as well. John rolled his eyes at Greg's showboat maneuver. Nevertheless, Ann was impressed and invited the two to join her at the table. Without hesitation,

Greg sat down beside her and John followed suit. John couldn't believe it, but Mrs. Frazier was flirting with his best friend.

Greg went on to tell her about his work as an attorney, and Ann seemed to be very interested.

"Actually, I'm in the market for an attorney," she said. "Do you practice all types of law, or do you specialize in just one area?"

"Mrs. Frazier, my practice is one where I do everything. *If* I need help, which is unlikely, I would call in the best specialist to help."

Ann turned to John and asked, "Is your friend full of himself, or is he just that good?"

"Both," John replied, and they all had a good laugh.

"Well, it looks like I've found myself an attorney," she said.

Greg beamed from ear to ear. He pulled out a business card from his suit pocket, but before giving it to her, he turned it over and wrote his home number.

"Here you are, Mrs. Frazier."

"Please, from now on you are to call me Ann."

She flagged down a server and ordered an expensive bottle of champagne, along with three fluted glasses.

"This calls for a celebration."

"Too bad you didn't bring those fancy cigars from New York," Greg lamented.

John quickly stood up.

"If you'll excuse me, I just left something in the car."

He ran outside to the parking lot to retrieve the gift for Greg, but as soon as he reached his car, he realized he had just left his boss's wife alone with one of the most lecherous men west of the Mississippi. John practically sprinted back to the table with the gift and was relieved to see the two laughing hysterically. At least Greg hadn't offended her—yet.

"Actually," John said, reaching into his coat and retrieving a long box, "you might be in luck."

John handed the gift to Greg and he quickly opened it to reveal a box of Davidoff cigars.

Greg beamed.

"Do you mind if we light up?" he asked Ann.

"Oh, of course not. Besides, I have to run."

She dropped a couple of crisp one-hundred-dollar bills on the table.

"That should take care of it, boys. I'll give your secretary a ring tomorrow, Greg. John, it was nice to see you."

As she walked away, he had to give his friend a swat to stop him from ogling his boss's wife.

"Strictly business, man. I don't want you to get me into trouble," John warned.

"You've always been a worrywart!" Greg responded.

"Just remember who she is."

"Of course," he replied, and stuck out his hand. "And I will never forget who introduced me to my gorgeous future wife."

 # EIGHT

After a night spent tossing and turning, worrying about Greg's antics with Mr. Frazier's wife, John was startled by Ryan Starr's arrival. He heard the car horn at exactly eight thirty a.m., and again as he was locking the back door to meet him. *This is going to be a long day,* John thought and waved to Ryan, perched in the driver's seat of a brand-new Grand Prix.

John opened the door and took a moment to absorb the interior—soft leather seats, custom stitching and detailing. It was a fine display.

"Too much action last night?" Ryan sneered.

"Starr, you are one sick SOB," John replied as Ryan pulled out of the driveway.

"We're gonna swing by a local teaching institute. I want to catch one of the Residents if we can," Ryan explained.

"So . . . what do you and your two sons do for fun around here?" John asked.

A big grin came over Ryan's face as he answered.

"Couple years ago, me and the wife built a log cabin on the lake. Pretty close to Chuck's, as a matter of fact."

John noticed that Ryan always referred to his boss as Chuck, never "Mr. Frazier," as he so often used. He stored this away for future reference.

"Just bought a brand-new, high-performance motorboat and a pair of Jet Skis," Ryan continued. "Also got a few vintage 'Vettes. Three from the early sixties, fully restored to their original condition. Always on the lookout for a new Corvette."

"What, do you have your own oil well in Texas?" John joked.

Ryan just chuckled.

"It's been a good run with Chalk Pharma. Matter of fact, the wife and I just built a home in Leawood for $650K. All this, and my wife gets to stay at home with the kids—that is, when they're not at Johnson County Prep. Can't complain, really."

If John were a cartoon, his eyes would have been dollar signs. He couldn't believe the enormous wealth of his coworker. For a moment, he was able to put his anxiety aside and rejoice in the future.

"What about you?" Ryan asked. "Got a woman with a lust for the good life?"

John was happy to talk about Sara. The very thought of her made his heart palpitate. Even though they had been seeing each other for several weeks, the butterflies had yet to wear off.

"Just met someone, actually," he replied. "I don't really know her spending habits, but I sure enjoy spending money on her. Bought her a $2,500 white gold, four-carat tennis bracelet while I was out in New Jersey. I haven't given it to her yet, but I'm hoping the look on her face when I do will be enough to erase the memory of that price tag!"

"I hear you, man," Ryan agreed.

They had reached the hospital by now, and as they pulled into a parking spot, John considered the possibility that diamond tennis bracelets were only the beginning.

****

It took Ryan only a moment to catch up with the Resident and speak briefly with him. Afterward, the two headed to their second call of the day, a retail pharmacy. Ryan explained that the store was part of a small, local chain of pharmacies called RX Health, and that the owner of the chain works out of the building they were about to visit.

"The owner's name is Scott," Ryan said. "Chuck and I call him 'FlatScott,' as in, his ass is as flat as a pancake. You'll see," he chuckled.

Inside the pharmacy, they quickly went to the back room of the store. John was amazed at all the boxes that evidently had pharmaceuticals in them. John felt dizzy amidst it all. There must have been a lifetime supply of medicine in that room—for the entire state of Missouri!

At the far end of the room stood a man who fit the description of FlatScott: The figure was devoid of a derriere and smiling from ear to ear. It appeared this man had unbounded energy and vitality as he rushed to greet John and Ryan.

"Chuck told me you'd be bringing in a new recruit," said Scott as he slapped John on the back.

"He's our *new rep*," Ryan said, emphasizing these last two words. "Technical terms, you know."

Scott appeared confused, but finally nodded and said, "Oh, that's right, chief. New rep."

John shook his hand, but really, he was wondering why the conversation seemed so strained between the two men when Ryan had been calling on Scott for several years. He wasn't too worried, though. FlatScott was one of those people who you couldn't help but like. It was no wonder he owned five pharmacies, all of which were prosperous.

"Welcome to the business," he said and released John's hand.

The three men chatted briefly, mostly about Ryan's new water equipment. John wasn't surprised to hear about Scott's own taste for the good life, but the excess of it all still amazed him. After they caught up on their most recent purchases, Ryan announced their departure.

"In that case, boys," Scott began, "could you take inventory of the Chalk products behind the counter? Knock yourself out and let me know if I need to put any orders in before I'm completely out."

John followed Ryan as he looked over the shelves containing the drugs. Ryan picked up a 500-tablet bottle of Faxlot. The bottle had a bright, colorful blue-and-white label. He turned to the pharmacy tech at the front counter.

"Are you seeing a lot of scripts for Faxlot?" he asked.

"Yeah, we're actually seeing quite a few scripts. It's only been out for a few days, but health-care providers seem to know about it," the pharmacy tech replied.

"Thanks," Ryan said and put the bottle back on the shelf.

Ryan went back to Scott's office and informed him that there was no need to put down any of their products on his want list.

"Looks like our new competitor, Faxlot, is really moving," Ryan observed.

"Sure is! And its usage is only going to go up," Scott answered.

"Say, what's the cost per pill?" he asked.

"Four bucks."

A big grin spread across Ryan's face.

"Thanks again, FlatScott. See you next time."

And the two headed back to the parking lot.

Once they got back to the car, Ryan debriefed John on his first retail pharmacy call.

"Pharmacy intelligence is critical to being successful in pharmaceutical sales," Ryan said. "Even today, with all the data collected on physicians' pharmaceutical preferences, one can still learn a lot on pharmacy calls."

John already knew this, of course. After the rigorous training session in New Jersey, he was probably more up to date on sales strategies than his seasoned comrade.

"Our next stop is a family-practice clinic," Ryan continued. "But before we get there, I want to explain the purpose of pharmaceutical samples. This is according to the man Chuck, himself. As you can see, like our competitor Faxlot, all companies will make sure their representatives have plenty of samples when they're introducing a new product on the market. That way, physicians can give them out freely."

"What is this, 'How to Sample 101'?" John joked.

Ryan looked at him sternly.

"This isn't a joke," he said. "When a drug is used for an acute situation, then the physician usually won't give a patient samples, but will instead write a prescription. On the other hand, for a patient who has a chronic condition like arthritis, the physician may want to give a patient two weeks to a month's worth of free samples. That way, they can see if the patient tolerates the drug and if it's effective. Now, there are a few physicians who will abuse the patient-sample privilege, but overall, they are very responsible."

"Got it," John replied.

But really, as they drove on in silence, he wondered exactly why he was telling him what he already knew.

****

They arrived at the medical clinic and Ryan led the way. Before they walked through the entryway, Ryan stopped John and proclaimed, "Now you'll see the master work his magic."

Ryan walked on, and John rolled his eyes before following him to the front desk. Ryan pulled out pens and scratch pads with the names of their products inscribed on them, and quickly handed them to the receptionist, whose nametag read: "Betty."

"I see you got a new guy there," Betty remarked. She turned to John and said, "Watch out for this one; he's a real troublemaker."

Ryan laughed.

"Don't listen to her, John, she roots for the Tigers!" he said, referring to the ultimate KU rivals, the University of Missouri Tigers.

Ryan led them back to the lab area, where he would wait to see all of the clinic's physicians. Over the next thirty minutes, Ryan saw each doctor for about five minutes, pitching at least two of Chalk Pharma's products to each one.

John was impressed by Ryan's extensive knowledge of the medical aspects of their products. Any and all questions the physicians had, Ryan handled with ease. His skills made John realize that he had a long way to go before he would be an equally effective pharmaceutical rep. A pharmacy degree was the first step, but being a top rep like Ryan would require learning some new skills.

Before leaving the clinic, Ryan announced they had one last stop to make. He led John back to an eight-by-ten-foot room with floor-to-ceiling shelving filled with samples from pharmaceutical reps. This room could accommodate a behemoth amount of pharmaceutical samples.

Ryan caught the look of wonder on John's face.

"Have you ever seen such a stash of pharmaceuticals in all your life?" he asked.

"Do most clinics have this many samples?" John inquired.

"Some have more, some have less. They're the grease to the wheels, in terms of sales."

Ryan opened his leather bag and started replacing samples that were running low.

After restocking the shelves with their samples, he turned to John and said, "Let's get that signature now."

They walked back out to the lab room and waited for the residing physician to sign off on the samples they had just left. Once they returned to the car, Ryan lectured John on the importance of entering into the computer the exact number of samples distributed, as well as getting the doctor's signature.

John already knew this, of course. He was well aware that all reps had to take inventories of their samples that were left over each month and most of the time, stored at their homes. Most importantly, all reps had to abide by the FDA guidelines regarding the storage of samples. On top of that, everything had to balance out on a monthly basis.

"Don't worry," Ryan said. "Chuck doesn't expect you to be as good as a seasoned pro like me, right off the bat. But don't forget that Chuck expects you to play by his rules. As long as you're a team player and work hard, you'll do just fine. On the other hand, go against Chuck, and your ass will be out in the street looking in. The man's been with the company for twenty-five years and has a lot of clout."

Though John had heard this warning before, the news was no less distressing. Again, his face betrayed him. After one glance at his passenger, Ryan swiftly changed his tune.

"But you've got nothing to worry about, kid. Chuck likes you a helluva lot. Said you'd fit into our district like family."

His cell phone began to ring, and he bent down and picked it up.

John figured it was Mr. Frazier as Ryan went into detail on their calls earlier in the morning. He was sure of it when he heard Ryan tell the listener that Faxlot was on the market and going for four dollars per pill. Before he hung up, Mr. Frazier must have cracked a joke because Ryan roared with laughter.

"So what was that all about?" John asked.

"Oh nothing. Business as usual," he replied.

John thought it was a rather curt reply, but again elected silence over confrontation.

"Oh, and the boss won't be making it for lunch," Ryan added. "Got tied up in business elsewhere."

John was actually relieved by the news. The hours with Ryan were starting to grate on him and all he wanted was to get through the rest of the day and get back into his lady's arms. Although he felt like he was definitely missing out on something, he was willing to put his misgivings aside—at least for the time being.

# NINE

Since Chuck was no longer joining them for lunch, John and Ryan grabbed a quick burger at Sonic before taking off for their next call. John was getting a taste of most aspects of the business—the clinic, the pharmacy, and now they would visit a nursing home. Ryan was the current representative for nursing homes in the greater Kansas City area, but the plan was for John to eventually take over some of the locations to lessen the burden on Ryan.

After spending half the day in the car, John felt as if he knew everything about his new colleague and any scrap of chitchat had been long spent. All except for one burning question he'd had since training class in New Jersey.

"So . . . ," John began, trying his best to act natural. "How did that woman I replaced . . . what was her name? Beth Beacon?"

Ryan interrupted, "One dumb bitch that won't be missed."

John was startled by his interjection, but continued with his question.

"How did she die?"

"Her own damn fault, that's how."

"Why is that?"

Ryan let out an exasperated sigh.

"Went off a cliff in the Ozarks. She was coming back from a district meeting at night. Everybody reasoned that she fell asleep at the wheel. I don't think it could have been mechanical issues because she had a company car that was only a year-or-so old and looked like it was in mint condition. So it was her own damn fault! But Chuck told me that the Highway Patrol report said that they found evidence that her brakes had failed. The company and her family did not seek any litigation activity because the company records indicated the car was in excellent shape. Personally, I think that dumb bitch fell asleep coming back late at night."

He went on to tell John about how she was married, but had no kids, so her husband had received a rather charitable sum from Chalk Pharma's life insurance policy. He laughed darkly and said he saw the husband a few months after her death in a new silver Mercedes. The man had made out like a bandit.

"She was a terrible sales rep, anyway. Chuck would have fired her if she hadn't beaten him to the chase and killed herself. Probably better she went off the cliff anyway."

His words hung over John. He knew this guy was strange, but the way Ryan spoke about such a tragic accident made him out to be a complete psycho. John wondered what else time would reveal about the Chalk Pharma group.

****

Ryan and John quickly made a call on the director of nursing at a nursing home. Ryan checked to make sure the retail pharmacy was fulfilling all their obligations concerning Chalk Pharmaceuticals' applicable products.

Sometimes the representative had to call on the retail pharmacies dispensing the drugs in order to carry out this task. Ryan advised John that it was unnecessary to call on the retail pharmacy unless there was a particular problem or issue. RX Health had the contract with this particular nursing home, so FlatScott made sure everything ran smoothly.

RX Health had contracts with multiple nursing homes in the Kansas City area. Of course, the majority of residents were on some kind of medication.

"Man, you could make a killing brokering directly to the patients," John joked. "Just cut out the middle man."

"Yes, a killing," Ryan agreed.

John realized that his coworker might have taken him seriously.

"But that would be illegal, of course."

Ryan turned and looked at him for a moment, sizing him up as if for the first time.

"Let's continue," he said, and led John down the hallway.

****

While Ryan and John made their sales call, Ann Frazier was keeping her appointment with Greg across town. Despite the array of knockouts Greg kept as secretaries, Ann was by far the most beautiful woman to grace his law office. Dressed in a body-conscious blue skirt and matching high-heeled shoes, she looked more like a woman on her first date than one attending to an apparently serious legal matter.

"So, how can I help you, Ann?" Greg asked from behind his desk.

Almost on cue, she burst into tears. Greg didn't know what to do, or if it was his fault. He decided his best bet was to remain silent and offer her some tissue. After a few moments, she managed to speak.

"I hope this is confidential," she said, her voice uneven from the sobbing. "It is of the utmost importance that you don't discuss this with anyone outside the office. Not even your best friend."

Greg raised his hands reassuringly.

"I never have, and never will, break attorney–client privilege."

He buzzed his secretary and asked for a cup of hot, herbal tea. By the time the tea arrived, Ann had calmed down even more and began to talk about why she was there.

"I'm here for two reasons. First, I should say that I brought a lot of assets to my marriage. And even though Chuck made me sign a prenup, I never protected my own assets in the agreement."

Although there was no pretext to this information, Greg knew where she was going. He also knew that it was best to play dumb in these matters and asked for formality's sake, "Why are you concerned with protecting your assets now?"

"When I married Chuck, I thought that I was marrying an honest businessman. But I now have reason to believe that he is the opposite—corrupt and evil. He's a wicked man."

It was all she managed to get out before bursting into tears again.

This time, Greg was shocked. He had guessed that she was unhappy in the marriage—the lonesome dinners, her eagerness to make contact with him—but he had no idea just how far the problem extended.

"What has changed your mind about your husband?" he asked.

Ann shifted in her chair uneasily before answering.

"A few weeks ago, my husband told me to be careful about what I say on the home phone. He said there's a possibility that it might be bugged or something. But when I asked about it, he played it off as if it were just a common safety procedure."

Greg shook his head and was about to speak when she continued.

"I know that may seem inconclusive, but I have many other examples of this paranoia. I only worry that if he's sued in some type of civil suit, my assets might be in jeopardy."

Both Greg and Ann mulled over her words. Now that she had unloaded at least part of her burden on Greg, she seemed to relax a little more and sat back in her chair. But after a few moments, a cloud passed over her face once again.

"Secondly, well . . . " she trailed off, searching for the right words. "I'm afraid of my husband. We recently got into a big argument. I told him I wanted a divorce and he said that they'd be fishing my dead body out of the Missouri River before he gives me a divorce."

"And you're certain he was serious?" Greg asked.

No tears this time—Ann sat up straight, resolute.

"Dead serious. Greg, I can't stand the sight of him. It's all I can do to make up an excuse just so I don't have to sleep with the man."

Upon hearing this comment, Greg's ears perked up like a wolf on the hunt.

"Mrs. Frazier, I will look into the issue of protecting your assets." He leaned forward in his chair, gazing intently into Ann's watery eyes. "I only need you to do some homework and bring in all documents concerning your assets to our next meeting. As for your husband, there's not much I can do to protect you, aside from giving you moral support. However, if you ever feel threatened or fear he might be violent toward you, call the police immediately."

Ann agreed and left the office after making an appointment for the following week.

Now alone, Greg began to wonder exactly what his friend had gotten himself into with Chalk Pharmaceuticals. As he went over Ann's information, his mind went back to Sara's comment to John about Mr. Frazier's friend, Simple Simon. He decided it was time to call in a favor at his former place of employment.

He picked up the phone and dialed. The line rang once before the operator picked up and asked where he would like to direct his call.

"Assistant U.S. District Attorney, Jason Thorn, please," he requested.

The operator connected him with his secretary, who informed him that Mr. Thorn would be out of the office for the remainder of the week. Greg told her to leave him a message: "Call back ASAP."

 TEN

After a long day spent making office calls, John found comfort in the company of his beautiful woman and a fine bottle of wine. The two hadn't been able to spend much time together since his return—she was busy at the hospital, and he had been tied up with business—but at last they were able to enjoy a night together and John could finally give her that long, narrow box that had been burning a hole in his pocket. Sara nearly fainted when she opened it and saw the row of sparkling stones!

The next morning, John woke up and instead of rushing off to get ready for work, he lingered in bed and watched the woman he now knew was his soul mate. She slumbered peacefully, with the tennis bracelet still around her wrist.

"I can see you, you know. I have eyes in the back of my head," she murmured.

"I don't believe you," John teased.

"And why is that?"

"Because if you really had eyes in the back of your head, you would see that it's 7:40."

Her eyes shot wide open and she leaped out of bed.

"I'm late!" she yelled.

John chuckled as he watched her scramble to the bathroom to get ready. He quickly put himself together too.

Later, as John kissed Sara good-bye in the driveway and patted her firm behind, he asked, "When will I see you again?"

"Depends. Are you asking me or my ass?"

John assured her he loved the whole package and helped her into her car before getting into his own. The warmth of her good-bye lasted only a moment before he realized what lay ahead of him. With a pang of anxiety, John pulled out of his driveway; he was working with Chuck Frazier today.

****

As he pulled up to his boss's house, he marveled at the Colonial-style home. It was located just a few blocks away from where Ewing Kauffman, owner of the Kansas City Royals and chairman of the board of Marion Laboratories, lived. The neighborhood was in Mission Hills, an upscale suburb of Kansas City, where the average house started at several million dollars.

John walked up to the ornate front door and rang the doorbell. A few moments later, beautiful Ann appeared in a silky, pink nightgown that left little to the imagination. She was about to speak when Chuck snuck up from behind and startled her with a kiss on the back of her neck.

John was hoping for an invitation to check out the home, but by the awkward look on Ann's face, he realized that it wasn't the right time to ask.

"Let's hit the road, rookie," Chuck said cheerfully as he strode past John. John nodded good-bye to Ann and ran after his boss.

Along with his laptop case, Chuck carried a brown bag, folded in half. Chuck caught John looking at the bag and laughingly told him that it was not his lunch, but offered no further explanation.

"We're going to my investment partner's home first, which is over by the City Museum," he said, and quickly gave him directions.

Although he didn't call him by name, John knew exactly whom he meant by "business partner"; he was referring to Simple Simon.

It took them close to twenty minutes to get there, a length of time during which John's anxiety grew more and more as he thought of Simple Simon and his creepy nurse. Once they arrived, however, Chuck instructed him to wait in the car.

John watched him walk away until he was out of sight and then, while reaching over to his console to find his sunglasses, he noticed Chuck's laptop case. *That's funny*, he thought. *Chuck left his laptop case, but took the brown bag with him.* He tried to resist temptation, but finally curiosity got the better of him and he unzipped a corner of the bag. It was just as he thought: a laptop, nothing suspicious whatsoever. But now he wondered what exactly was in the brown bag. He was even more perplexed when Chuck returned thirty minutes later empty-handed.

John waited to start the engine again, expecting some sort of commentary on what he had been up to, but he received none—only instructions.

"Head down Hangar Street. We'll make a joint sales call," Chuck said.

John obeyed, though his mind was now reeling at the thought of making a sales call with him. He'd always been an intimidating figure.

****

As they entered the hospital together, Chuck told John not to worry. The doctor who they were going to see was an old friend of his.

John could not believe it, but as they entered the hospital to go to a family practitioner's clinic, John heard Chuck holler at an older man in a white lab coat, "Dr. Marriott, how are you today?"

The man approached them with an extended hand and introduced himself to John as Dr. Marriott.

"Are you gentlemen coming to see me?" he asked.

Chuck replied that they were just on their way to make a call on him. Dr. Marriott asked if it was OK if they gave their presentation in the hallway because he was getting ready to assist in a surgery.

"Go for it," Chuck told John.

John gave a rapid—not to mention nervous—presentation to Dr. Marriott.

When he was finished, he asked, "So, Doctor, does your clinic need any of our samples?"

Dr. Marriot said that he was set. He added that the clinic would be remodeled over the next month, and so they should hold off on their calls for a while.

"Well, John," he said, "it was a pleasure meeting you. Drop by in a month and maybe we can get you in with some of my colleagues."

The doctor shook hands with both men and then strolled away down the corridor.

Once the doctor was out of earshot, Chuck turned to John and asked, "How does it feel to make your first call with me in your own territory?"

"I'm just glad it's over," John confessed. Chuck laughed, slapped him on the back, and made his way toward the exit.

As they walked back, Chuck reminded him to enter the call into the Chalk Pharma database. Once they reached the car, the first thing John did was pull up Dr. Marriott's profile on his computer and input the information on their call that day.

They made several more calls on physicians and pharmacies throughout the day, so that by the time John dropped Chuck off at home at five thirty, he was ready to collapse onto the sofa at his duplex. In fact, he thought he might invite Sara over so they could collapse together.

****

The alarm clock blared and John awoke, naked next to Sara and in a panic. Today would be his first day flying solo. The phone rang and forced him out of his frenzy. He reached over and picked it up, only to hear Joe Arnold greet him on the other end.

"Hey, John, hope I didn't wake ya. Just wanted to see how you're getting along with the new job."

How thoughtful, John thought. *Maybe he's not such an asshole after all.*

John rolled out of bed, careful not to wake Sara, who had slept through the call, and walked to a place where he wouldn't be heard.

"Actually, Joe, maybe I shouldn't even ask you this question, but . . . " he trailed off.

"What is it? John, I hope you know that you can come to me in confidence on any matter, especially if it pertains to Chalk Pharma."

John hesitated, but then continued, "Yesterday I dropped Chuck off at Simon's house. He didn't return for maybe thirty minutes."

"Yeah," Joe prompted.

"What is the relationship between those two? Can I ask you that?"

"Sure, no problem, rookie," he replied. "The three of us go way back. Chuck and Simon have quite a few joint business ventures together. They own some apartment complexes and bought land that sold for big bucks to developers. They also own a ranch. That's where the boys go hunting and fishing. You can go too, John. Any time you want, just ask Chuck ahead of time."

"Wow, I guess I must be working for a multimillionaire!" John exclaimed.

Joe chuckled at his statement and said, "That's a fair assumption, rookie. But you'd never know it by his clothes, right? I mean, the man has no color coordination. I bet he buys them right off the rack at Kmart."

Not wanting to insult either his boss or his coworker, John reluctantly laughed and went on to ask Joe if he knew FlatScott.

"FlatScott? Yeah, I know FlatScott. We've all been friends for about thirty years now. Real nice guy. But don't let the nickname fool you; he's a very serious businessman underneath."

John heard a noise in the kitchen. He walked down the hallway and saw that Sara, dressed in one of his oversized Drake T-shirts, had woken up and was now making coffee. As she bent down to get a filter from the bottom cabinet, she offered him a very compelling view of her very skimpy underwear.

Sara noticed John watching and whispered, "Which would you like this morning: coffee, tea, or me?"

"Thanks for the info, Joe. Gotta run. See you soon."

John hung up the phone and turned his attention to more pressing matters.

****

John's time in the field went off without a hitch as he became more comfortable in the life of a pharmaceutical rep. But he had been so busy on the job that he hadn't been able to catch up with his best friend since they'd had dinner with Mrs. Frazier.

When Greg finally did call, it came as no coincidence that she was the first topic of conversation. Greg told him that Ann had mysteriously cancelled her second appointment with him and had not yet called to reschedule.

"And hey, don't tell her husband she sought counsel. My ass would be grass," he said.

Other than those comments, Greg remained completely confidential about Ann's visit to his office.

"Uh, duh!" John shot back.

If his boss found out, not only would Greg be toast, but he was pretty damn sure that it would come back around to haunt him too. And like Ryan and Joe warned, Chuck was not a man to cross.

 # ELEVEN

The drizzling rain obscured the view of the road through John's Grand Prix as he made his way back home after a long day of making calls in his territory. Each day he felt more confident in his skills as his conviction settled in that he had found the perfect career match. And now he was on his way to see his buddy for some celebratory brandy and cigars. He had only one thought: *How could life get any better?*

He looked forward to seeing what felt like his long-lost friend that evening. But there was something about Greg's voice when he called and asked him to meet him in his office that made him think it wouldn't all be laughter and fine liquor. Then again, the man was known for his propensity to bullshit, so it was just as likely that it was typical Greg trying to pull John's leg once again.

As John pulled into the parking lot, he saw Greg already waiting at the door, waving to him. Half expecting him to have a can of silly string behind his back, John approached him with jocular caution.

"Ready to meet some dirty-legged hens, my friend?" John asked.

However, he stopped in his tracks when he saw that Greg's face remained stony.

"Hey, what's up? I thought all this stoicism was just an act," John said.

Greg glanced around the parking lot like an eagle at his perch.

"Afraid not. Let's go into my office and I'll explain." He ushered John inside and, after reactivating the building's alarm, followed him to his office.

John walked around the office, observing the mundane objects that littered the room: a golf calendar, a beer stein from Greg's fraternity days, a framed photograph from their weekend trip to Branson three summers back. Anything to distract him from what he was beginning to realize would be unpleasant news. But why the discretion? Why couldn't they go over this on the phone before they were to have a night out on the town?

Greg took a seat behind his desk and gestured for John to take his own on the other side.

"So, Milkman, how is the pharmaceutical world treating you?"

His question seemed so nonchalant compared to his initial grave demeanor, which confused John more than ever.

"Couldn't be better," he replied.

Greg's face became stony once more. This time, John couldn't keep the observation to himself.

"Hey, man, I thought you'd be happy to hear that I'm digging the new job."

Greg looked up, surprised.

"Oh, it's not that. Sure, I'm happy for you. It's just . . . " he trailed off.

"Just what?" John asked. "Please, just get on with it. The sooner you tell me, the better you'll feel."

The two remained in silence for a few moments longer before Greg finally spoke.

"About a week ago, I called a former boss of mine, Jason Thorne. He's an assistant district attorney here, in Missouri. You want to know why?"

It was a moment before John realized Greg was waiting for an answer.

"Oh—why?" John asked.

"Ann Frazier."

"My boss's wife? But why?"

"We had our first meeting not too long ago, and she said a few interesting things. Just like Sara had some interesting things to say to you a few weeks ago."

John still didn't know what this was leading up to.

"Cut to the chase, Greg."

"Jason Thorne investigates crime in Kansas City. And what's the number-one crime organization in KC?"

"The mob," John murmured.

Greg slowly nodded.

"Mr. Thorne has requested a private meeting with the two of us tomorrow evening. But he's far more interested in what you might have to say."

"Oh shit," John replied. "Do you think this has something to do with Simple Simon and Mr. Frazier?"

"Well, I can't confirm it, but if I had to guess, I'd say you hit the nail right on the head."

As John sank further into his chair, Greg explained that he should not get upset. This was only to be a friendly conversation between the men. Most importantly, he was not to tell anyone about it, and keep all the details confidential, even from Sara.

At the end of it all, the two men had traded places. Greg, all smiles, broke out the brandy and cigars as John stared into the distance in shock. The liquor helped to loosen him up, but he couldn't help but feel like he was on the precipice of something far more dangerous than he cared to become involved with.

As Greg poured John another round, he said, "Give me a dollar."

John looked up at him, perplexed, as he continued.

"Aw, come on, it's not so I can buy myself a glow-in-the-dark rubber. This way, you can claim attorney–client privilege from this night forward."

"I thought they only did that in movies!" John replied, and humored his friend.

Greg took the dollar and went back into lawyer mode.

"Have you done anything illegal since going to work for Chalk Pharma?"

"Not a damn thing, as far as I know."

Greg glanced at his watch. "Well, it's getting late and I don't think either of us are in the mood to go out on the town. What do you say we call it a night, meet back here tomorrow at the same time, and drive over to Thorne's office?"

John agreed, and the two called it a night and went their own separate ways.

****

The evening dragged on because John was filled with anxiety. John returned to Sara, who was miffed by his alcohol-and-cigar-smoke breath, but was happy to see him nonetheless. Her warm embrace offered some comfort throughout the night, as John tossed and turned, struggling with the uncertainty of what the coming day would bring.

At work, he tried his best to keep busy until it was time to pick up Greg to go to the meeting with Thorne. It was a short trip to the office, and during the fifteen-minute drive, Greg briefed John on what to expect.

He knew Jason Thorne from his internship during the summer between his second and third year of law school at the district attorney's office in Kansas City. Consequently, he knew that he was a guy they could trust. His boss was head of the Federal Organized Crime Strike Force in Kansas City, so it was in their best interest to fully cooperate with any requests they might have.

Once they arrived at the building, Greg guided them to the eleventh floor, where he had worked just a few summers prior.

"Reminds me that I'm just as poor now as I was then," Greg lamented.

John couldn't help but chuckle at his comment.

Etched-glass doors announced the entrance to the *U.S. Attorney's Office*. They walked through, and John was surprised to see that not only was there no lobby, but there was also no receptionist at the front desk.

Greg looked down the hallway and hollered, "Anybody home?"

A nasally voice called back, "Greg, buddy! Is that you?"

The owner of the voice appeared through a doorway down the hall. Greg and John walked down to join him. With dark-rimmed glasses and a square head, the man reminded John of the cartoon character Poindexter.

"Jason Thorne," the man said as he shook hands with John. "Nice to meet ya, even if you are friends with this skeeze over here."

"Please, don't hold it against me," John joked.

"Look, I'm glad you two have something to joke about, but I'd like to know what the hell is going on," Greg interrupted.

Thorne threw up his hands.

"Whoa, buddy, easy there. Everyone is back in the conference room. Come on, I'll take you there."

As Thorne turned to lead them down the hall, Greg looked over his shoulder and John mouthed a silent *"oh fuck."* Greg smiled and walked confidently into the conference room.

Upon entering the room, Thorne made introductions to the people who were already seated around the long table. There was Shirley Phillips, a deputy U.S. attorney who worked for Jason; Tom James, an FBI agent; and Ted Bishop, a DEA agent.

Just listening to their titles made John's heart race. He was relieved when they cordially asked him to sit down and offered him a beverage. John accepted a Diet Coke, but what he really needed was a stiff drink.

Greg took charge of the situation.

"Will there be any minutes or tape recordings of this meeting?" he asked.

Thorne assured him that there would be no need to record their meeting. It was, after all, just a friendly conversation.

"If this is a conference between friends, then why do I feel so nervous?" John interjected.

Nervous laughs echoed across the table, and everyone settled in for the real talk to begin. Shirley spoke first.

"John, there's no need to be nervous or upset. We are not questioning your activities; on the contrary, we are asking for your help."

Thorne jumped in.

"We all appreciate your willingness to come over, given the circumstances. We know that we've been rather tight-lipped about the pretense of this meeting, but we assure you, it's only for your own safety."

"Look, thanks for the pleasantries," Greg interjected, "but we've got a reservation at the Plaza III at eight, so can we get down to business?"

DEA Agent Ted Bishop spoke directly to John this time.

"I'm sure you know what is meant when one refers to the pharmaceutical gray market."

Greg smirked and said, "I don't have the foggiest idea what the term means."

John remained silent and allowed Agent Bishop to continue speaking.

"Pharmaceuticals disappear from their proper legal sources, and are then illegally resold on what is called the gray market. Nobody knows the size of this market, but it exists across the country. Pharmaceuticals disappear each year, but they always surface somewhere else."

Greg remained calm and collected, but his voice was much more gruff when he spoke.

"Are you implying that my client has been involved in illegally diverting pharmaceuticals?"

"Not at all," Agent Bishop shot back. "I just want to be sure that we are all on the same page when it comes to the gray market and illegal pharmaceuticals distribution."

"Then what the hell is John doing here?"

John almost pissed his pants when he heard the words escape his friend's mouth. Not only was Greg getting out of hand, but John was also almost certain that very serious trouble loomed ahead.

"Keep a lid on it, Greg," Thorne warned.

"Well, come on, let's quit beating around the bush!" Greg looked around the table. "Someone give us the skinny."

FBI Agent Tom James cleared his throat and said, "As you all probably already know, organized crime has evolved a great deal. These corrupt individuals are no longer just involved in the old-time crap such as racketeering, prostitution, and extortion. Now, the mob, or whatever you want to call it, is becoming more and more sophisticated in their schemes. Some of this is due to the fact that they are better educated. Some have even become respected professionals in honorable fields of business. Kansas City runs the scale, from soldiers all the way up to the boss."

Throughout his explanation, Agent James had been turning pieces of paper, as if reading off of them. But at this point, he stopped and looked up at John before continuing.

"And in this case, we all know who the mob boss is. We know who pulls the strings. He goes by Simple Simon."

# TWELVE

The mere mention of his boss's "associate" made John choke on his Diet Coke.

Tom noticed his reaction and commented, "That's right, John. Chuck Frazier's close friend just so happens to be the undisputed kingpin of the Kansas City mob. We also know that he is a throwback from the once nationally feared Kansas City Outfit. Simple Simon is somewhere between eighty and ninety years old. We are uncertain of his exact age, but he moved from Sicily to Staten Island as a young boy. He came to Kansas City in the late 1920s.

"Simple Simon was a reputed mob enforcer back in the mid-1930s, during the Pendergast political-machine era. In the 1960s, the Kansas City Outfit even had an investment in the Tropicana Casino in Las Vegas. They were taking an exorbitant amount of money out of the Casino. As time went on, he eventually became the mob boss of the Outfit. We're uncertain on the exact date when he became the head man in KC, but we believe it was in the mid-1970s. In fact, we think it occurred after the River Quay explosion, the mob was suspected of. The Outfit is the only criminal group in the city to this day with a full range of illegal activities."

Bishop continued, "We understand that even to this day, he brags about being on a first-name basis with Harry Truman during the Pendergast era."

"If I remember my history right, didn't the Pendergast machine have a lot to do with Truman's political career?" Greg interrupted.

"No doubt about it," Tom responded. "Even though most historians suggest otherwise."

After listening to the agents carry on about the mob, John finally spoke.

"Mr. James, I appreciate the history lesson, but what makes you believe that my boss is anything more than a friend to Simple Simon?"

Greg smiled smugly at his friend's response.

Bishop's answer wiped the smile right off: "Simple Simon doesn't make friends."

Suddenly, the room grew sullen, as if someone had turned a dimming switch.

"John," Bishop continued, "we have no doubt that Chuck Frazier is involved in a complex scheme to divert pharmaceuticals into the gray market with Simple Simon."

"Bullshit!" John yelled. "There is no way that your information could be accurate. I know the man. He teaches Sunday school, for God's sake."

Jason Thorne had remained silent for the past fifteen minutes, and so his voice startled John when he said, "Shirley, why don't you tell John what we know."

"Shouldn't we get his commitment to help us first?" she questioned.

"I don't think John will commit to anything if he doesn't have all of the facts."

Greg leaned forward on the table and said, "You know, we're still in the room. We can hear what you're saying."

Jason looked slightly embarrassed by his lack of decorum.

"Sorry, gentleman. It's just that we want to make sure we don't tell John too much if he decides not to help us. This is sensitive information, you understand."

Greg was about to respond when Thorne continued, "However, we can see that John has a great deal of respect for Chuck. We're going to have to divulge a lot of what we know to get his support."

"How about we call it a night and get our acts together for a meeting in the future?" Greg asked. "I think my client is in a state of shock over this whole ordeal you're trying to involve him in, and he needs some time to absorb it all."

"That would be no problem," Shirley replied. "We just need your assurance that all of this will be kept strictly confidential."

"And Greg," Jason added, "I'd like to see you for a couple minutes out in the hallway. Privately."

He nodded toward the door, and Greg followed him.

****

Once they were outside, Jason lowered his voice.

"You have to make sure this meeting remains highly confidential. It is our belief that a pharmaceutical rep named Beth

Beacon, who worked for Chuck Frazier, was murdered in what was made to look like a car accident. She was planning on turning Frazier and some of her coworkers into the DEA and this office. Apparently, she thought something was up. We don't know how they found out about her intentions, but the fact remains: They did. And she was a very cautious person. She knew not to discuss this with anybody in-house. I tell you, she had the *fear of God* in her when it came to her boss."

Jason allowed this to sink in for a moment before continuing.

"If these people get wind that John has been in communication with us, then his life could be in serious danger."

By this time, Greg's face was bright red. Sweat rolled down his forehead.

"How could you put my client in this type of danger?" he demanded.

"Your client is in no danger so long as you keep everything confidential. Even so, he's in no danger until he agrees to help us. In which case, we will do everything we can to assure his safety."

This news was just too much. Greg simply shook his head and walked back into the room.

He looked at John and said, "Let's get out of here."

While the others remained at the table, perplexed, Thorne chased after the two down the hall.

"I'd like to set up another meeting in the next few days!" he shouted.

"I don't think we have anything more to discuss," Greg responded as he threw open the etched-glass doors.

"OK, so when Attorney Greg Clarke returns, please tell him to give me a call so we can have another meeting."

Greg got the last word as he ushered his friend out the door: "Fuck you, Jason!"

Jason threw up his hands and watched their departure. John wasn't surprised that he tolerated Greg's behavior; he was probably used to it after spending the summer in the same office. He knew that Greg had one hell of a temper and that whatever he had ignited with Greg would take a while to cool off.

****

John and Greg listened to the hum of the engine as they drove to the Plaza III for their long-anticipated steaks. But after the shakedown in the DA's office, neither was in the mood for much of anything, except for hitting a punching bag.

"Let's at least have a few drinks and discuss what happened. You'll find your appetite when you see the filet mignon," Greg said.

They arrived at the restaurant and the hostess took them back to a corner booth, tucked away from the din of the other patrons. As soon as Greg caught sight of their server, he ordered for both of them a double Crown Royal on the rocks and Chivas Regal shots with Bud Light chasers. When the drinks arrived, Greg tossed his back before explaining to John what had happened in the hallway.

By the end of it, John's face registered total disbelief.

Greg tried to reassure him by saying, "Don't flip out. This may or may not be true. After all, if they knew for sure that Chuck Frazier was involved in a murder, then they would have charged him long ago."

John settled back in the booth, gripping his third Chivas.

"Then again," Greg continued, "it might be time for you to find a new job."

Greg smiled at his touch of humor, but John bristled.

"I'm not giving up this job, man! I've only been there for a brief period of time, and what major pharmaceutical company would hire me after leaving another company after such a short period of time? Not to mention, my student loans, debt from my furniture, and the gifts I gave Sara. I'm in over my head by at least $150,000."

"Well, you could go out and just get a retail-pharmacist job," Greg suggested.

"Fuck that! It would take me at least a few years in a position like that before I would even begin to earn this kind of money. And forget about bonuses for the most part."

Greg looked at his menu in silence, contemplating his friend's situation.

"I guess you should stay with Chalk Pharma for another six months. That'll give you enough time and experience to qualify for another job. For the time being, keep a low profile. No job is worth getting killed. Just mind your own business and don't let anyone know about your suspicions."

"Thanks for the advice," John replied sarcastically. He glanced at the menu and realized that he was actually famished. The stress of the day had zapped him of his energy, and he was ready to be replenished. They both ordered the large filet along with a few more rounds of drinks.

****

Afterward, as was tradition, they lit up cigars for the ride home. It was difficult for John to use the lighter at first, and even more difficult to meet the flame with the end of his cigar after their numerous nightcaps.

"Sure would like to poke Ann Frazier," Greg muttered.

John's mind was also cloudy, but he was still struck by his friend's perverted mind.

"I can't believe that at a time like this, you're thinking about having sex with my boss's wife, of all people."

"Well, hell, it's not like Frazier can have me killed or anything."

It took a moment for his comment to sink in, but when it did, both men doubled over laughing. They stretched themselves over the hood of the car for support. Their laughter subsided and quiet took its place as the men looked up at the starry night sky, intermittently clouded by the smoke of their cigars.

The two sat in silence for quite some time, until their cigars were spent and their boozy fog had lifted. Once they gathered their wits, Greg drove John back to his car.

"Give me a call tomorrow, Milkman! I'm seeing some serious court action in the near future representing you. I'd better start training now!"

John laughed as his friend drove off, but once the taillights faded into the distance, he realized that he was alone and didn't like it. He fumbled with his keys, quickly turning the ignition and following Greg's path. As he drove home, he hoped more than ever that Sara would be able to join him tonight.

****

The red, blinking light on his answering machine calmed John's nerves. He dropped his keys on the kitchen table and hit the play button. To his surprise and dismay, it was Chuck Frazier's voice bellowing out of the machine, not his lady's. It took him a moment to recognize his boss's voice, as it lacked its usual warmth.

"Meet me for breakfast. Fairmont at eight thirty a.m., tomorrow."

John hit the button again and finally heard Sara's voice.

"Hey, hon, some of the girls are going out to party after work. I'm gonna tag along. I'll see you soon. Miss you!"

Dreary and disappointed, John set his alarm clock and passed out on his bed.

****

The ringing alarm forced John out of sleep the next morning and into his intolerable hangover. He reached to shut off the alarm and nearly fell back asleep in the following silence. But just as he was about to drift off, his boss's voice echoed in his head, reminding him that he had an eight-thirty-a.m. call time.

The thought of this made his eyes flutter open. It took him several moments to calm the spinning ceiling and his frayed nerves before he could get out of bed. He took a quick, hot shower, threw on his suit, and ran out the door for the Fairmont.

****

Sara had quit her part-time job at the coffee shop. But before she had quit, she told John that Chuck had breakfast two or three times a week with Simple Simon, so he was extremely relieved to arrive and see Chuck alone at his usual table. However, something else made John's stomach suddenly turn into knots: Chuck Frazier looked angry.

John nervously approached the table. Chuck curtly told him to sit down, and he obeyed. His tone and demeanor bewildered John. But now, with a sinking feeling, he could see how Chuck could actually be much more duplicitous than he'd initially thought. And John was about to learn firsthand the extent to which this was true.

THIRTEEN

A thin manila envelope rested beside Chuck's elbow on the table. As John sat down across from him, he slid it across.

"I'd like you to read the contents of that file," Chuck said quietly.

John slowly retrieved it, and tried to steady his hands as he opened the file. There was a computer printout with his name at the top. Below, the title read: "Calls on Deceased Doctors in Territory #1285."

It was John's territory, and he couldn't believe his eyes when he saw the error that his boss was pointing out: The report listed a call on one *deceased* Dr. Marriott.

"I'm sorry, I'm a bit confused," John confessed. When he looked up to meet his boss's eyes, he knew that Chuck had already made up his mind about John's guilt.

"Tell me what you're confused about," he replied.

"Well, the date appears to be correct. I did call on Dr. Marriott at that time and place. But I can assure you, he was walking and talking. It wasn't too long after you and I saw him. I didn't even know that he was sick."

Chuck leaned forward and spoke slowly.

"Dr. Marriott died a few days after we called on him. So you're mistaken. You must have confused another physician with Dr. Marriott."

"But I know that was Dr. Marriott. There's no way I could have mistaken him." John's quivering voice betrayed his inner panic.

"I'm telling you, it wasn't him," Chuck snapped. "It's my responsibility to inform you that you could be terminated for this blunder."

The color drained from John's face as he tried to think of a rational explanation.

"It was an honest mistake, sir!"

"Calm down!" Chuck cut him off. "I'm sure I can fix it with the company. You'll get a warning, but at least you won't be terminated. They'll send you a letter within the next couple of days. Just a formality, but if I can get in touch with the director of sales today, I can iron it out in no time. Normally, you'd be on the chopping block, but some of these guys owe me a favor or two, so I can pull some strings."

A wave of relief washed over John.

"Thank you, sir. And I apologize for the—"

"Think nothing of it, John. This little misdemeanor aside, you're developing into a fine rep. You'll have a good career with Chalk Pharma." Chuck said this with a smile, but his face shifted back to his initial, grave expression before continuing. "At least, you'd better, because if you ever got fired from us, no other company will take ya. So you can understand how imperative it is that you play by the rules from here on out."

"Of course, sir. Like I said, it was an honest mistake. And it will never happen again."

Finally, Chuck's stony gaze gave way to a grin, and he punched John on the shoulder. "I'm sure it won't. But don't forget: You owe me big-time now!"

"Of course," John replied. "But let me ask you, will this go on my permanent record?"

Chuck let out a deep laugh before telling him that it would, but it was no reason to worry; he had far worse infractions in his own file.

"Now if you'll excuse me," he said, "I think I'll try to reach that director of sales now. Order for me?"

"Actually, sir, I don't have much of an appetite anymore."

Mr. Frazier smiled and said, "John, it'll all be taken care of. You'll receive the letter at your home office, and that will be the end of it. Aside from what you owe me, of course."

This time it was John who was laughing. Chuck returned a smile and shook his hand as John stood up from the booth.

"Keep doing a good job. Don't let this get to you."

John nodded his head and left the coffee shop. But before leaving, he quickly glanced around for any sign of an elderly man in a black hat.

****

Despite the jarring news, John continued with his day as he normally would, making a couple of sales calls and following up on paperwork. Throughout his work, he vacillated between being grateful for having a boss who would bail him out of a bad

97

situation and feeling unable to understand how he had gotten himself into such a situation to begin with.

He knew Dr. Marriott. John may have still been learning the sales lingo that Ryan Starr had already mastered, but one thing that John was most definitely skilled at was remembering faces. He had seen the doctor with Chuck, had connected his face with the name that Chuck pronounced as they shook hands—the same name and face as when John went back there a second time on his own. Or so he'd thought. The call had been brief, not to mention, he'd had a lot on his mind after his meeting at the DA's office.

But none of that matters now, John thought. Mr. Frazier would see to it that he received nothing more than a slap on the wrist.

Nevertheless, he couldn't suppress his nausea, and at around three in the afternoon, he decided to head home. The slap on the wrist had already arrived via his fax machine. It was a three-paragraph letter from the director of sales.

Subject line: "Presentation to Deceased Physician, Bill Marriott."

John read the first paragraph:

It has come to my knowledge that you made a call on one Dr. Bill Marriott after he was deceased. I have received an account of the incident from Charles Frazier. Your call-reporting activity involving Dr. Marriott was incorrect, as you listed the call after his passing. A call on a deceased physician demonstrates inattention to detail, which is critical to being a successful pharmaceutical sales representative for Chalk Pharmaceuticals. This memorandum serves to clarify the importance that Chalk

Pharma places on the accuracy of reporting calls. Further infractions will not be tolerated. Should you repeat this inaccuracy, you may be terminated or face alternate disciplinary action.

John looked at the address line and saw that the letter had not only been copied to Chuck Frazier, but also to the marketing director and regional manager. It was enough to receive a letter of that nature, but they had to publicly humiliate him too. He was only a rookie, and yet he was already making a name for himself—and not one he wanted to stand by.

Suddenly, his vision of an English manor house in Ireland, filled with artifacts and antiques, seemed unimaginable. Maybe he hadn't gotten fired, but what if this was just the beginning of these innocent mistakes? He felt like he had no control. If he lost his job, he would spend the rest of his days working off the enormous debt of his college education and loans in exchange for the good life. He may even have to ask Sara to give the bracelet back.

Sara! The thought of what he would tell her hadn't even dawned on him. Just as they were beginning to grow close, he'd jeopardized his future. Would she still be interested in a dumbshit salesman who calls on dead doctors?

The room seemed to shrink and rise ten degrees in temperature. John doubled over, his abdomen cramping into knots. He barely made it to the bathroom before his body relieved itself of the lunch he had not enjoyed earlier.

After what seemed like an eternity, John dropped to the cool, bathroom floor and wished for sleep, and with sleep, clarity. How had he ruined his shot at making his dreams come true?

****

After the nausea subsided, John tried to reach Greg at the office. The call went straight to voicemail. He called again—straight to voicemail. Rather than leave him a message, he decided to pay his friend a personal visit.

It was after office hours when he arrived, but the front door was still unlocked so he walked straight back to Greg's office.

"Hey, Milkman, where ya been?" Greg called out, as if he were expecting John. He sat behind his desk, perusing a magazine.

"Hell and back," he replied. "Where were you? I tried calling you a million times."

"What are you talking about? I've been here the whole—oh, wait."

Greg stood up and walked out to the reception area. After a moment, he came back in. "New secretary," he explained. "Best ass I've ever seen, but, boy, is she dumb. Left the phone off the hook. Third time it's happened this week."

"Sorry to hear about your troubles," John responded, and reached into a vanilla file folder that he had brought along with him. He brought out a piece of paper and tossed it onto Greg's desk.

Greg sat down and read aloud.

"Official warning?"

He continued reading and when he was finished, looked up and asked, "What the hell is this about? Calling on dead doctors?"

"It's bullshit. I'm sure that I called on the same Dr. Marriott as when Chuck was with me. In fact, Chuck and Dr. Marriott were old friends. But this morning, Chuck told me that the guy died soon after our visit."

Greg stared at John for a moment, taking it all in, before bursting into uncontrollable laughter. John threw his hands up and headed for the door.

"Wait! Wait," Greg said through gasps of air. "Come back and have a drink."

He went to his personal liquor cabinet and brought out a bottle of Crown Royal. He poured two large shots and brought one to his buddy, as well as a handwritten note.

"From my secretary," he said, as he handed both to John.

The message was short:

*Greg, your buddy is getting framed. Be smart and give
me a call for another meeting.
—Jason Thorne.*

When John finished reading, he collapsed backward in his chair. Greg poured himself another shot and held it up to John.

"May your ups and downs be between the sheets, not with your fucking job!"

Only Greg could have brought a smile to John's face at that moment. His face brightened and he reached for his own shot glass.

"So what the hell does Thorne mean?" John asked.

"I'm just guessing," Greg responded, "but from what you showed me today, I think Thorne's office is tapping Frazier's phone. They probably overheard Frazier talking about giving you that letter and setting up this whole Dr. Dead issue."

John looked confused.

"But whom would he be in cahoots with? Ryan Starr is his favorite rep. I wonder which phone they tapped. They must know who was involved, if they got the information."

"Who knows what phone they used to discuss framing you. Point is, the Feds were listening, so they probably have even more information," Greg replied.

Just hours before, John was thinking about how lucky he was to at least have his boss on his side, but now there was evidence that he was anything but. He couldn't accept this news without questioning it a bit further.

"But Chuck was the one who agreed to step in and save my job. He talked to the director of sales for me so I wouldn't get fired," John reasoned.

Greg looked at John with pity. He couldn't be the one to burst his bubble.

"I think Jason Thorne might be able to give us the answers we're looking for," he replied. Then, almost mockingly, Greg assumed his sullen, attorney demeanor. "With your permission," he said, "I would like to set up another meeting with Thorne and his people."

"Let's seal it with another shot," John replied.

"Deal," he answered and got up for another round.

# FOURTEEN

Jason Thorne jumped at the opportunity to get John back into his office, and within twenty four hours, Greg and his client found themselves face-to-face with the same board of keepers of the peace. Shirley Phillips, Tom James, and Ted Bishop all sat around the long table, each with their own file and legal pad, and all looking equally eager to get down to business.

"Well, boys, I'm glad to see that you've decided to cooperate," Thorne began.

"Wait a minute," Greg interrupted. "Let's get one thing straight: We haven't agreed to do anything but get some answers."

Thorne thought better than to respond to Greg's typical hardheaded approach.

"We're glad that you've agreed to a second meeting," he continued. "I'm curious, did you bring a copy of the warning letter?"

"Oh, you mean the blatant evidence that you have a tap on Chuck Frazier's phone?" Greg taunted.

Thorne smirked in response.

"John," he said, "didn't Chalk Pharma give you a cell phone to use for business?"

John nodded, suddenly very aware that he needed to choose his words wisely.

"And doesn't everybody under, and including, Chuck Frazier, have the same kind of phone?"

Again, John nodded.

Thorne turned to Greg and asked him what he made of these facts. Greg stared down at the table and formulated his thoughts before he spoke.

"It suggests to me that you have been scanning and monitoring Chuck Frazier's cell phone, as well as other members of his district. I imagine you even have Mr. Frazier's home-office phone bugged through a court order."

"Precisely," Thorne replied, rapping the table with his fist. "Greg, you sure you don't want to come back and work for me full-time?"

Greg laughed and replied, "If you could pay me the kind of money I'm worth, then maybe I'll consider it."

Thorne laughed in return, and the tension lifted from the room. Gone were the introductory formalities. Now it was more like two old friends offering trade secrets.

Thorne told them that they would hear more about the telephone conversations later, and again asked for a copy of the warning letter. Greg opened his briefcase and presented it to the table. Once more, that self-satisfied grin returned to Thorne's face, as if he'd found the last egg on the Easter hunt. He held up the letter and pointed at the top.

"As you both probably realize," he began, "Chuck Frazier set John up with this dead-doctor business."

All of the shame and anxiety came rushing back to John, and he forced his eyes away from the letter. Greg looked at him reassuringly, but it was all John could do to sit and listen to Thorne make his point.

"The truth is," Thorne said, "one Dr. Marriott is, in fact, deceased. Frazier was a close friend of this man and knew about his terminal illness. Stage 4 colon cancer. He knew that he only had a few days left to live." Thorne set the paper down and paused for a moment to take a long sip from his coffee cup.

"Before Dr. Marriott died," he continued, "Frazier brought in an imposter to meet with them so that John could enter a call on the fake doctor while they were together. Later, without Chuck, John revisited the fake doctor and again entered the call. What you didn't know, John, was that between the two calls, the real Dr. Marriott had died. Of course, Frazier had known the approximate time and date that John was going to call on the imposter. He knows every move you make from the itinerary and schedule that all district members fax in to him on a weekly basis."

John was shocked. He couldn't believe that someone could have so easily pulled the wool over his eyes.

"I didn't even give it a second thought," he said. "But now that I do think of it, it was funny how he told me to wait to see the other physicians on my next trip due to the renovations taking place at the clinic. And he told me not to restock the samples because they were 'set for now.' Then, the second time I made a call on him, he was waiting for me in the hall and told me the exact same thing."

The table remained quiet as the news sunk in. Finally, John continued speaking.

"Why would Mr. Frazier do this to me?" he asked.

"Because Chuck Frazier is a cocksucker," Greg answered.

Everyone in the room broke out in laughter, but regained composure when Thorne cut in.

"No," he said. "Because your boss needed to frame you so he could get you under his thumb. It was a way to bring you under his control. He knew that if he bailed you out of a situation that could have cost you your job, you would feel indebted to him—willing to do anything the man who saved your career asks. *And* he's a cocksucker."

This explanation did not sit well with Greg.

"Does Frazier really think that this would buy John's loyalty?" he asked. "That he would participate in illegal activity for this— let's face it—*small* favor?"

"I'd say so," Thorne answered. "Or if that failed, then he could tell John about how he framed him and that he could easily do it again, but make it more serious. Frazier felt he could control John by either gaining his loyalty after rescuing his job, or by playing hardball to keep him in line. One way or the other, John would become a partner in his illegal activities."

Up until now, the conversation had been exclusively between the three men. But finally, another person spoke. It was Shirley Phillips, whose sympathetic face made up for Thorne's lack of tact.

"John, you need to realize that you were handpicked for this job. Not just because you were qualified, but because of other attributes that Chuck knew he could use to his advantage," she said.

John looked up.

"What the hell are you talking about?" he asked.

Thorne followed Phillips's cue and went around to John's chair and patted him on the shoulder. "Have patience. I know this is confusing and difficult to process."

John wanted to squirm away from his gesture, but instead, politely nodded.

After a moment, Shirley spoke again.

"One of the attributes that Chuck looks for when hiring new reps is someone who is really financially oriented. Money hungry."

John looked up at Shirley after she spoke this last part and the two held each other's gaze.

"Isn't it true," she continued, "that you have purchased rather expensive clothes and furniture lately? Isn't it also true that you have a large, outstanding debt with Drake?" Shirley opened the folder in front of her and skimmed through the pages. When she found the one she was looking for, she stopped, and read from the page. "You told Frazier that you 'do not want to be just another pharmacist making a good living, but a high-roller, making over six figures after my first year out of school'?"

"In other words," Thorne continued, "Chuck knew all along that your main motivation for choosing a career in pharmaceutical sales was the amount of money you would rake in."

John looked around the room, suddenly feeling helpless against these accusations. After all, they were completely true. And now he didn't feel like the person who would help put the bad guy in the slammer, but rather, the poor fool in the interrogation room.

From the end of the table, Ted Bishop chimed in.

"The bottom line, John, is that Frazier has been planning this from the beginning. In simple terms, this means that he's going to use you. However, if you're willing to play ball for Chuck, then you will certainly become very wealthy. The only people he knows will get hurt are those who don't play ball for him."

Greg held up his hand in protest.

"Wait a minute. I don't know if I'm alone in this, but I don't completely understand all of the illegal activities that Chuck Frazier has been carrying out. It was my belief that it has to do with diverting pharmaceuticals into the gray market, as well as the suspicion that he had something to do with the murder of one of his former young, female reps. But what are we really talking about?" he asked.

Tom James took the lead on this question and answered, "Unfortunately, we don't even know all of the illegal activities concerning drug diversion. We are aware of many federal laws that Frazier and others have broken during their involvement with the process of diverting pharmaceuticals; however, we don't know the full breadth and depth of their operation."

"Which is why we need you," Thorne interjected, pointing a finger at John. "We believe this whole drug-diversion operation is like a three-legged stool. One leg involves buying pharmaceuticals at deeply discounted prices for alleged nursing-home use and ultimate entry into the gray market. The second leg of the stool involves selling other companies' pharmaceutical samples taken from physicians' offices and selling them into the gray market. The third leg involves selling Chalk Pharma's own samples into the gray market. How all this is being accomplished is still unknown to us. We need someone from the inside to complete the puzzle."

Ted Bishop pointed out that under the Prescription Drug Marketing Act of 1987, any individual who violates the sales restrictions is subject to felony charges, and if convicted, could face up to ten years in prison, as well as a fine of up to $250,000. Violators could also be subject to civil penalties.

"One of the other big issues involved with this situation," Shirley Phillips said, "is the fraud committed by those misleading drug manufacturers who think they're selling their pharmaceuticals for use at a nursing home."

Phillips was about to continue when Ted Bishop once again asserted himself.

"I'm mainly concerned with the PDMA because I'm with the DEA."

"But the fraudulent activities involved with this case are equally important," Shirley abruptly cut in.

They were about to continue their argument when Thorne jumped in to announce that he would take over the roundtable discussion. But before he could do so, Greg interrupted.

"Why would my client be willing to get further involved in this whole situation? He could just walk away from it. Quit his job. I mean, John is a good citizen, and a great guy, but it doesn't make sense for John to get involved if it entails him dealing with the likes of Frazier or the mob."

Greg then turned to John and addressed him.

"My advice to you, as a friend and client, would be to quit this job and forget about the whole mess—"

"It's about patriotism," Thorne interrupted, his face reddening.

"Forget about that," Ted Bishop interjected. "It's pretty simple." Bishop leaned forward and told Greg, "We can make your client a very wealthy young man."

"You must all think I'm some kind of money whore!" John exclaimed.

"Relax, buddy. Let's hear what he has to say," Greg cautioned.

Ted waited for the din to die down and said, "Under the PDMA, as an enticement for individuals to help enforce the law, anyone who provides information that leads to another person's arrest and conviction for selling, buying, or trading drug samples will receive half of the criminal fine collected for this. The maximum one can receive is $125,000 for each person convicted."

John considered this for a moment and was about to speak when Ted continued, "We believe that there are somewhere between five to ten people who are involved in the scheme to divert samples. That includes Chuck and a number of his reps, pharmacists, and mafia figures."

Now John looked up. He wasn't sure what to say. The open discussion about his eagerness to earn money shamed him. He had never had his character framed in such a light before and he felt deeply guilty. Then again, facts were facts: Money made the world go 'round, and money made it possible for John to lead the life he'd always dreamed of. But before he could give any definitive answer, Bishop announced it was time for a break. Greg ushered John into Thorne's office for a private meeting, leaving Thorne and the rest to discuss what had happened.

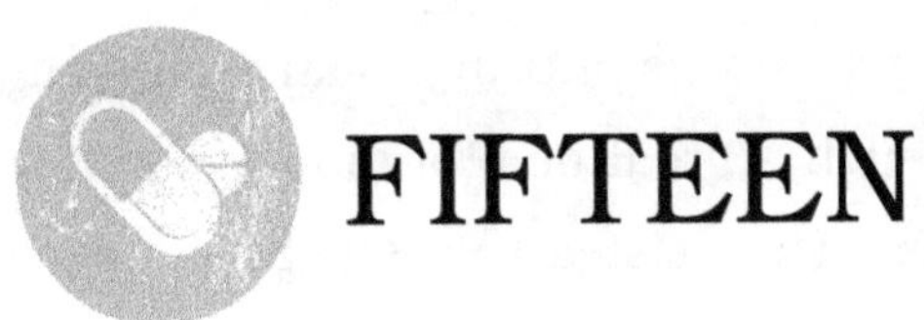 # FIFTEEN

John had to practically run to keep up with Greg as he rushed into Jason Thorne's office. As soon as they were in, Greg slammed the door and ordered John to take a seat in Thorne's large, overstuffed chair behind the desk. The office matched Thorne's Poindexter look: standard, run-of-the-mill decor, government-issued furnishings, and not a speck of character to speak of. John was relieved by the blandness of it all. After the meeting he'd just had, the last thing he needed was added stimuli.

After a few moments of silence, Greg finally said, "Milkman, this job of yours has got you between a rock and a hard place. I want you to remember that you can totally walk away from this, go out and start all over."

John considered his friend's words.

"I studied the Prescription Drug Marketing Act of 1987. They were absolutely correct in what they told us."

Greg took in a deep breath as if preparing to answer, but John held up his hand and continued.

"If we decide to jump into this mess, I want to make sure that you will get a percentage of anything I receive."

"And if you decide to get further involved," Greg said, "you'll earn every cent you make."

John couldn't believe his friend was putting up an argument, especially since it involved such a great deal of money—money that Greg could certainly use. He insisted that Greg get a slice of the pie, but Greg protested.

"You're putting the cart before the horse! Let's just decide whether or not we're going to get involved in the first place."

The biggest concern was that, with John's increasing involvement, he might end up in some type of federal government witness-protection program. It was likely that the mob would want to retaliate against him, so it would be essential to keep John's identity a secret.

"We can cut a deal with the prosecutors and DEA so that you don't have to testify or give any depositions to a federal grand jury. Snitches earn themselves bad reputations, I would imagine, especially when it leads to the incarceration of people involved in the drug-diversion scam. Plus, we can get the DEA to agree that the money you receive for your help will be dropped into a trust fund. That would make it nearly impossible for anyone to ever be able to trace the money to the source: you."

Greg had an attorney he knew who could get them the information regarding setting up a trust. Paramount to John was only that he had immediate access to this trust. After all, he had a chunk of debt to his name. But he didn't want those government officials in the other room thinking that he would help them because of the money.

If he were to get further involved, it would be because he was a decent individual and a pharmacist. His ethics as a pharmacist were strong, and he would always follow state and federal guidelines, no matter what. Not to mention, the drugs that entered the gray market were potentially lethal. If there were some sort of recall on any particular drug, those that entered the gray market would go unnoticed. Furthermore, part of the drugs passed around ran the risk of being outdated.

"Listen, John," Greg said. "I get the whole patriotic act, but I still think we should keep an open mind regarding your involvement. If we decide to get further involved, we should still make sure that our demands are met."

John stood up and extended his hand to Greg. They exchanged a firm handshake before cracking a smile and pulling each other in for a brief embrace. It was time to rejoin the group.

****

As they walked down the hall, they could see Shirley Phillips leaning against the projector in the conference room, accentuating the "s" curve her figure cut in her pencil skirt and dark blazer.

"Ever been with a black woman?" Greg whispered. "Woo-wee!" John shot Greg a dirty look.

"What? I'm just trying to add a little levity to the situation. Try to laugh a little."

The group members seated themselves around the table once again, and John was offered another drink.

"I'll take a Diet Dr. Pepper," he quipped. "Because I call on dead doctors that have no pep."

Thorne looked at him sideways.

"Diet Dr. Pepper it is, then," he said, and grabbed a can for him.

Go figure, he wouldn't get a joke, John thought.

After he slid it across the table to John, Thorne asked, "So, have you gentlemen come to a decision?"

"No. No, we have not," Greg said. "If we are going to rock and roll, there will be certain conditions that have to be met."

"Before we talk about any conditions, I think I should tell you more about those telephone conversations I mentioned earlier."

Thorne looked at John, then Greg, then at the rest of the table, waiting for protest.

When no one spoke, Thorne continued.

"Just for your information, the Electronic Communications Privacy Act of 1986 makes listening in and tapping or divulging the contents of wireless cellular calls a federal crime. Therefore, we got a court order to scan and monitor Frazier's cell and office phone."

When Greg and John looked at him blankly, Thorne said, "Most people are under the false impression that law-enforcement officials don't have the monitoring equipment to scan cell phones."

Thorne stood up and walked over to the projector stand. He reached under it and brought up a tape recorder, already loaded with whatever media they were about to listen to.

"I'm going to play a tape recording from Frazier's office phone. The conversation took place between Frazier and Ryan Starr."

Thorne then hit the start button and the digital tape began. John immediately recognized his boss's voice.

"Starr, how'd your day go, working with Johnny Boy?"

"Found out that John Boy has a spending habit. Especially when it comes to the ladies—particularly, his girlfriend, Sara."

John's heart sank when he heard her name. Not only was he in deep shit, but now the love of his life would be dragged into this? It was bad enough, and it just got worse.

"Good! Goood!" Chuck responded.

"John bought her a very high-priced tennis bracelet when the shit was supposed to be training in New Jersey."

"And here I thought he'd spent it on booze and prostitutes!"

Chuck cracked up at his joke. Ryan followed with an inappropriately loud laugh.

"Also, John was getting nosy about your lifestyle. I ended up telling him about my boys attending private school, and how my wife is a homemaker. I told the kid that I built an expensive house in Leawood and a log cabin in the Ozarks, and bought a new motorboat and Jet Skis. Oh, and don't forget about my 'Vettes!"

Chuck cracked up again and asked Ryan, *"What do you think of all that?"*

"I think that John's eyes are as big as silver dollars."

"Yes, that's right." Chuck continued laughing. *"John likes money more than he likes us."*

Thorne stopped the tape abruptly and turned to John. "See?" he asked. "See what we were talking about? You were handpicked!"

Suddenly, the color of John's face more aptly lent itself to the nickname "Cherry Tomato," rather than "Milkman." Thorne continued playing the tape.

Ryan's voice came on again.

"There's definitely going to be a lot of stock bottles of Faxlot and regular Faxlot samples in the clinics."

"Perfect!" Chuck confirmed.

Ryan snorted and asked, *"Is it getting close to the time we spring the dead-doctor plan?"*

"No. We just have to wait a little longer. Shit, the man has to at least be on his deathbed first!" He laughed again, each time growing in magnitude. *"I'm talking to Mrs. Marriott once a week to get a report as to how he's progressing."*

"Our John Boy really is green," Starr commented.

"Green like the color of money!" Chuck bawled. *"Now I want you to continue to make friends with him."*

"Will do. Hey, Boss—I told him never to fuck with Chuck."

"Never hurts to put the fear of God in his mind," Chuck replied. *"Now keep your eyes and ears open about Faxlot. I'll talk to you in a couple of days."*

Thorne once again stopped the recorder, only to observe John, who was even redder than before.

Then John said something that surprised everyone: "Those cocksuckers!"

Greg hadn't seen John this angry since a couple of years ago when they were playing basketball and some idiot undercut John as he was going in for a layup.

Thorne also sensed that he was slow to anger, and that this was definitely serious.

"Are you ready to kick some ass?" he asked John.

Before John could answer, Greg waved his hands in front of his face and exclaimed, "Whoa! Whoa!"

John shooed him off and gripped Thorne's hand.

As they shook hands, John looked Thorne straight in the eyes and said, "I want you and the group to understand something: I will not get involved with this whole mess because I am mad, or because of any financial rewards to me. If I decide to pursue these criminals, it will be because I am a pharmacist first, and a first-class citizen."

John explained what he had told Greg in Thorne's office. He explained what kinds of drugs go into the market, and the risks that are run in the absence of regulations. The team listened to him throughout the entirety of his speech, in awe that this otherwise mellow man could become so emotional.

"Does this mean you're on the team?" Thorne asked.

John nodded "yes" and the group applauded. Soon, everyone was up on his feet, shaking hands.

"Stop the presses!" Greg shouted, waving his hands. "Jason, before any commitments are made, like I said, there are certain conditions that we want before we commit to John's help."

Thorne looked at John, who was back to his pale, Milkman self, and agreed.

"My lawyer will tell you the conditions. If you people agree, we can go after these cocksuckers ASAP."

****

During their next bathroom break, John went to the can while Greg began listing off their working conditions. He reiterated his concern about how the mob might retaliate against

John. But to his surprise, they agreed to do everything they could do to keep John's identity secret. They agreed that he would not have to testify or give any depositions to a federal grand jury. They also agreed to always put John's best interests ahead of the case. Of course, Greg was suspicious as to whether or not they really meant that, and he was still worried about keeping John's identity a secret.

Their discussion was coming to a close as John was in the bathroom, zipping up his pants. He went to wash his hands in the sink.

Looking into the mirror, he said, almost reassuringly, "I sure hope the Milkman knows what he is getting into."

John couldn't believe how complicated his life had become in such a short period of time. It wasn't so long ago that all he had on his mind was chasing after Sara and having a great career in pharmaceutical sales. Somehow, he had a feeling that those days were gone forever and that it would be quite some time before his life would ever be that simple again.

****

John reentered the conference room in time to catch the end of Greg's explanation that they wanted a trust-fund set up for the financial rewards. Thorne was impressed by this idea and said that he would speak to one of their best trust attorneys within the Justice Department. Bishop added that he would have to speak with his DEA superiors to make sure they were on board with the idea. But even Tom James thought it would fly with the FBI.

"Sounds like you've got your head on straight, son," Bishop said to John.

Thorne stood up and announced that it was high time they adjourn the meeting until Friday afternoon. They'd have lunch catered and finalize the conditions of John's participation and then decide how to proceed. The deal had been struck.

SIXTEEN

John had left his duplex that morning unsure of what the future would hold. He returned to his duplex no less unsure, but with a newfound confidence. What his boss was doing was not only corrupt, but also endangered the lives of other people. Finally, he had a purpose—other than chasing the almighty dollar—to live for.

It was a relief to open his front door and reengage in the familiar activities of coming home. He threw his keys on the side table, kicked off his shoes at the front door, and walked over to the answering machine with its red, blinking light. He had only been gone for the afternoon, but there were several messages waiting for him.

The first message was from Ryan Starr.

"Hey, John, meet me for lunch at J. Alexander's in Johnson County. Leave me a voicemail confirming that you can make it."

John decided to address that later, and continued to the next message. The tension he had been holding in his shoulders since the night before eased as he heard Sara's voice.

"Hey, baby, when you get a chance, let me know if I'll ever see you again."

OK, so maybe she was pissed, but it was nice to hear her voice anyway.

The last message was from Chuck Frazier. He and Ryan must have consulted with each other, because he asked if it was possible for him to meet Ryan for lunch the next day. Once the beep sounded, indicating the end of the messages, John picked up the phone and left a message in both Ryan's and Chuck's mailboxes on Chalk Pharma's voicemail system to confirm their lunch meeting.

With that out of the way, he moved to more pressing matters. He once again picked up the phone, dialed, and listened. It seemed like an eternity before the line picked up.

"Hello?"

"Hey, cutie pie," John answered. He suddenly realized that it had been a couple days since they had last spoken—practically a couple of years when it came to Sara.

"Well, well. I was just about to send out the hounds. Didn't think I'd hear from you again," Sara said.

John wanted to confess everything that had happened, from the dead doctor to his cooperation with the DA's office, but instead, he simply said, "Sorry, I guess I've been working hard and studying new material at the library."

"Oh, so you found a sexy librarian. I get it."

Though she sounded aggravated, John knew she was only toying with him. A broad smile stretched across his face.

"Honey, bring your cute little ass over here and I'll put your fears to rest."

John knew by the sweet, low giggle on the other end that she was on board.

"I'll be there in twenty minutes," she said. "If you're sure you want me, that is."

Truthfully, John wasn't really in the mood. A long, hard day of questioning and tough decisions had wiped him clean of that. But he also knew that he needed one look at Sara sans clothing and the tide would turn.

"Twenty's too long. Make it now," he said, and hung up the phone.

****

John awoke in a daze. He wasn't quite sure how he had gotten to his bed, or how he'd woken up, but when the doorbell sounded several times, he realized that it was Sara and that he must have drifted off waiting for her to arrive.

He smoothed down his bed-ruffled hair in the mirror and went to the door. Through the peephole, he could barely make out her subtle form. He threw open the door and was nearly knocked over by her sheer sex appeal. Her hair was up in a high bun and she wore body-hugging blue jeans and a tight, white shirt with nothing underneath.

"Get over here," he commanded.

With a squeal, she leaped into his arms and he carried her into the living room. He set her down and gave her the once-over, landing on her full chest.

"Is it just me, or is it cold in here?" he joked.

Sara held his gaze and replied, "Give me a break. I haven't seen you for a while, and the girls have missed you."

John could barely contain himself. He couldn't keep his eyes off her as she led him back to the bedroom. They couldn't get there fast enough as far as he was concerned. Just as they reached the doorway and Sara began sliding up her shirt, exposing her smooth, flat abdomen, the phone rang. Suddenly, John found himself in the middle of a moral dilemma that made his time at Jason Thorne's office seem like small stuff.

Finally, he threw up his hands and yelled, "Crap."

Sara smoothed the front of his pants and said, "Baby, you can wait a little longer."

John looked at his caller ID and saw that it was Greg. *Of course it's Greg*, he thought bitterly. He answered the phone and caught Greg mid-sentence.

"Slow down, buddy. I can't understand you," John said.

Greg took a deep breath and started again.

"Ann Frazier just called me at home. She's coming to my office around lunchtime and we're going to the Plaza."

John took the cordless phone, walked into the bathroom, and shut the door.

"Listen, man," he said, "I've got some female company of my own."

Before Greg could give one of his usual, childish responses, John continued.

"Look, I'm meeting Ryan Starr for lunch tomorrow. Chuck Frazier even asked me to."

"Well, you know that if you find out anything important, then call me immediately tomorrow afternoon. If need be, I will call

Thorne to keep him and his legal staff posted on any possible illegal activity that might occur before Friday."

"OK, yeah. Will do," John replied.

"Guess I'll go then. I know when I'm not wanted. I'll let you have your romantic time with Sara, so go get your dipstick wet." Greg cracked up.

As John hit the "off" button, he could still hear his horndog friend laughing. He quickly placed the phone back onto its base and returned to the bedroom, where Sara was waiting.

"So what's her name?" she asked, stretched out on John's bed.

"I'll give you two clues: She has a foul mouth and a very hairy back."

To John's surprise, instead of responding with a clever quip, she stood up and unsnapped the top of her designer jeans.

She started to pull down her zipper when she said, "Did he ask if you were getting busy with your 'long-legged hen'?"

John let out a roar of laughter. He loved that Sara was adding his jargon to her vocabulary.

"Yeah, something like that," he said.

"I'm sorry, John, but I can't spend the night. I've got to go back home and get ready for the third shift at the hospital," she said, pulling one leg of her jeans off at a time.

"Well, it looks like my friend was right, after all. I am going to be awfully busy once you get your jeans off," John replied, and flicked the light switch.

****

The next morning, John busied himself with sales calls in the field and didn't stop until it was time to meet Ryan at J. Alexander's for lunch. He arrived on time, but Ryan was already seated in a corner booth waiting for John. As he slid his tall frame into the cushy booth, Ryan raved about the ground-chuck burgers they served.

"The best in the entire metro area!" he announced.

"I've never had the chance to eat here. It's such a long jaunt from the Plaza," John replied.

"Oh, that's right; I forgot you lived that far away."

Ryan signaled to the waiter and ordered for them: two iced teas, two ground-chuck burgers with cheddar cheese, and two fries.

They continued casually conversing about other restaurants in Kansas City, but when the food came, Ryan got down to business.

"I hear you have a problem calling on dead doctors," he began.

John glared at him with a look that could kill. His intimidating posture only made Ryan snicker, and he soon began to laugh so hard that John thought he might never stop.

Finally, John said, "You sure know how to kill someone's appetite."

"Don't worry about it, man. Lighten up. The Big Boss took care of the whole thing for you."

John could not believe this asshole was rubbing it in his face. Now that he knew that Ryan was in cahoots with Frazier in framing him, it took all the control he could muster to not call him out to his face. His mind drifted to what the hell they were planning now.

No sooner had John completed this thought than he realized Ryan was speaking to him again.

"Hello? Earth to Whitey?" he nagged. When John refocused his attention, he started over. "So I'm having a party Saturday afternoon."

John looked at him inquisitively.

"What kind of party is this?"

"Nothing, really," Ryan replied. "Chuck and I just decided that we're going to bring you into our confidence."

John's heart raced and he feared the worst. But he couldn't betray his inward anxiety to Ryan who, as far as he knew, still thought that John was a dummy concerning their alleged criminal actions.

"What does your confidence have to do with a party?" he asked.

Ryan chose his words carefully.

"This is a *special* kind of party," he said.

"Would you quit beating around the bush and get to the point," John demanded.

"Damn, John. I'm just inviting you to a shucking party."

"What the hell is a shucking party?" John asked.

"You'll find out when you get there. We just want you to come out and see what it's all about. Other members of our district will be there too. Joe Arnold, Mavis Turner, and others."

John tried his best to hide the bewildered look on his face, but it was of no use. Ryan picked up on his misgivings and lay on the heat.

"Unbelievable. Chuck just bailed you out of a situation that would have cost you your job. He saved your career. And now he specifically requests your presence, and you turn him down? What an amateur."

John felt stuck. He knew that it was inevitable. The whole point of the dead-doctor setup was to gain the leverage necessary to get him to participate in illegal activities. But he'd had no idea it would all happen so fast. He thought about his meeting with the Feds and was sure that Jason Thorne's office would want him to attend the party.

"Time and place?" John asked.

Ryan smiled and said that he would pick him up at one o'clock that afternoon and have him back by seven o'clock. The party was going to be at an old farmhouse that Frazier owned. Before leaving the restaurant, the two men shook hands and Ryan said he would pass along John's consent to Chuck.

"Plus," Ryan said, "make sure you don't tell anyone about the party. Above all, don't use the word *shucking* around anybody except those directly involved. It's just that no one else would understand."

John agreed, but as soon as he returned to his car, he said, "Shithead Ryan!" and picked up his phone to call Greg's office. Greg's secretary informed John that he was still out to lunch. He had forgotten that Greg was going out with Ann Frazier that afternoon, and it would be no surprise if he wasn't back until much, *much* later.

****

Greg and Ann had just started on their Irish coffee after lunch at the Classic Cup. Their talk had been casual throughout the meal. She'd told him about vacationing on the Mediterranean, and he'd told her about the golf tournament he and John played in every year. But finally, now that the plates were cleared and it was just the two of them and their drinks, Greg broke the ice.

"Ann, I've been wondering since you called me—why did you need to see me so quickly? I mean, you missed your previous appointment without so much as an explanation."

Instead of answering directly, Ann told him to finish his coffee and they'd go for a drive. Greg stood up, gulped down the whole cup, and announced he was ready. Ann nodded and led him out to her shiny, white BMW.

In the car, Greg was distracted by Ann's skirt inching up her thighs, showing just how leggy she really was. He thought she had noticed his eyes on her thighs because she seemed to wiggle into the seat, exposing even more as they pulled away from the curb. Finally, Greg remembered what the Milkman had told him and reminded himself that it was only wishful thinking. She was off-limits.

She drove them around the Plaza, then through Westport, and finally through the midtown area, where she broke down and began telling Greg about how much she detested her husband.

"I have to find a way to protect my assets that I brought into the marriage. I just don't know what will happen since I didn't sign a prenup."

Greg tried to explain, as he had before, that there were things that she could do legally now to protect her assets. Once the divorce was filed, he would be able to find out from Chuck's attorney whether or not he was going to try to go after her assets, and if so, on what grounds.

This seemed to calm her, at least for the time being. But both of them knew it offered limited comfort. There was still so much that was unknown. True, Ann knew that her husband was a badass, but did she know just how corrupt he really was? Furthermore, did the Federal Crime Strike Force? Greg could only wonder.

As they reentered the Plaza, they were only a couple blocks away from Greg's apartment. He innocently pointed north, in the general direction of his apartment, and the next thing he knew, Ann had turned her white Bimmer in the direction of his residence.

"Actually, my office is in the opposite direction," he began, but as she threw her head back and laughed, her strawberry-blonde hair blowing in the wind, he knew that it was no innocent mistake.

She looked at Greg with bedroom eyes.

"I want to know where you live just in case I have an anxiety attack and I need you to calm me down."

Greg's jaw muscle had tightened so much in excitement and anticipation that he couldn't respond. This woman was a client, and client–attorney relationships were frowned upon. So even though he desperately wanted to see what was under the rest of her silky skirt, he was relieved when Ann turned her car back around in the direction of Greg's office.

But now Greg had second thoughts. Had he just missed his one opportunity to hook up with an Ann Margaret lookalike?

"But I thought we were going to my apartment," he said.

Ann glanced at Greg.

"It would not be ladylike," she replied, and drove on.

Ann dropped him off at the office, and once more, he realized he was glad they'd never made it back to his apartment. Their relationship was still professional, and—as of yet—he hadn't muddled himself in Chuck Frazier's personal affairs.

He went into his office and reviewed his messages, including the one from John. Greg quickly picked up the phone and called him back. He heard all about John's lunch with Ryan, and assured John to not worry about it. They would tell Thorne at their scheduled lunch the next day.

"So," John finally asked, "how was your lunch with Ann?"

"Strictly legal, buddy!" Greg responded.

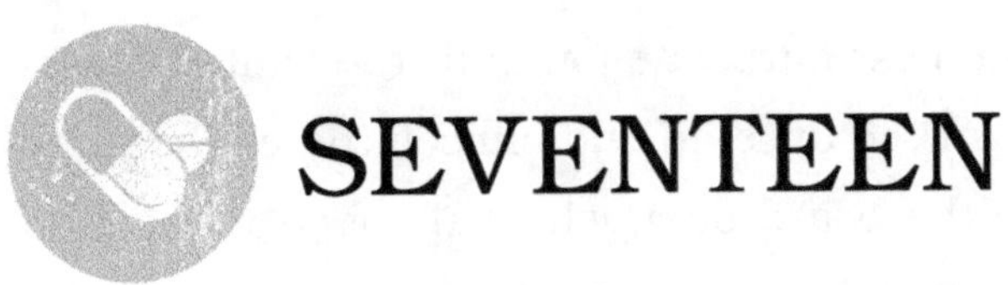# SEVENTEEN

$\mathbf{F}$riday morning went quickly for John, and before he knew it, he was pulling into the parking garage at 11:45 for the meeting with Jason Thorne and company. He arrived before Greg and waited for him in the first-floor lobby. Once Greg arrived, John rose from his seat to shake his friend's hand, but was surprised when Greg punched him playfully on the shoulder.

"Isn't it a great morning?" he beamed.

"Any words of advice?" John asked, glad to see his friend in a good mood, even if it was slightly mysterious. Greg told him to just play it by ear and tell them exactly what he had told him on the phone the day before. John was still perplexed by his friend's giddiness, and realized that he must still have had Ann Frazier on the mind.

John knew better than to ask Greg how things had gone, nor did he want to even know if anything was going on between his criminal boss's wife and his best friend, although he did enjoy the thought of someone screwing over Chuck Frazier. That asshole was the reason he was in the DA's office in the first place; he was the reason his whole future was now in jeopardy.

****

As they walked into Thorne's office, the aroma of Gates Bar-B-Q arrested their senses. Gates was a Kansas City institution, and one of the best barbecue joints in the United States. Suddenly, John wasn't so upset to find himself there. The receptionist led them to the boardroom, where the food was set out and Thorne and his people were waiting.

"Come on in, guys," Thorne yelled. "Grab some grub."

They followed suit and took a seat at the table. Shirley Phillips went around, filling cups with pink lemonade. When she filled Greg's cup, he smiled ear to ear and gave her a coy wink.

"What's the matter, Greg? Got something in your eye?" she asked.

"Only problem with my eye is that it's not big enough to take in all of your beauty."

She smiled and asked in a sweet, motherly voice, "Guess it's been a while, huh?"

John hit Greg on the back and told him to behave himself.

Shirley looked at John and said, "Honey, don't worry about it. In this setting, we hear all sorts of things from big-shot attorneys who are in private practice. They're the ones who make the *big* dollars, right?" She turned and looked Greg over. "But then again, Greg's shoes suggest otherwise."

A couple of other people at the table had now caught on and howled at Shirley's surly response. Greg couldn't leave it alone, and quickly formulated a smartass reply.

"Anytime you want to come over to my place and see an expensive bedroom set, just let me know."

Finally, Shirley showed disgust on her face and went back to pouring lemonade. But John noticed that when Shirley sat down at the front of the table, she discretely flipped Greg the bird. Greg ate it up.

Once everyone was seated and tackling their respective mounds of barbecue, Greg told the group that John had an important update that was pertinent to the case. John didn't get up, but he told the group that yesterday, he had been invited to a shucking party by Ryan Starr per the request of Chuck Frazier.

"What's a shucking party?" Thorne asked.

Ted Bishop answered for him.

"I'm very familiar with this type of party. Though it's really not a party at all—"

"Honestly, guys, I have no idea what this is all about," John interjected.

Before Ted could continue explaining, Shirley spoke up.

"I don't think it's a good idea to tell John what he will witness at a shucking party." The table looked at her with skepticism, and she continued. "After all, we want John to show how he would normally react to everything he would see at that party. Otherwise, they might think that John's reactions are not legitimate."

The table remained silent. Then, Thorne asked Greg and John to step out of the room for a moment. He had to find out what a shucking party was before they could make a final decision.

Approximately five minutes passed before John and Greg were invited back in.

Before Greg sat down, he asked, "What's for dessert?"

John just shook his head and realized that he wasn't asking for more food. He was looking directly at Shirley.

She snapped back, "There's no dessert, but with an appetite like that, I'm surprised you're so thin!"

"Me too," he replied. "I'm always going after something sweet."

John could not believe that his friend was behaving so unprofessionally. This was the most serious business he had ever found himself involved in, and Greg was still more concerned with chasing tail. Fortunately, John realized that he and Shirley were the only ones who realized what Greg actually meant.

Thorne finally spoke up.

"We've decided that John should just go to the shucking party on Saturday without any previous knowledge. We don't want to compromise his reaction to the situation. However, we want John to know that he doesn't have to worry about any personal-safety issues. It was the consensus of the group that we will get a court order quickly so that we can set up surveillance inside and outside the farmhouse."

"Are you sure it was Chuck Frazier's farmhouse that Starr set as the destination?" Bishop asked.

John confirmed the fact, and Thorne said that it would be easy for them to find out where the exact location was.

"And what if Frazier owns more than one farm with a farmhouse on it?" Greg demanded.

Thorne looked at Greg with disdain for a moment, but then a smile quickly formed and he said, "That's my boy! Always thinking two steps ahead."

Tom James would be handling the surveillance setup, so he said, "The Bureau already knows the location of this particular farmhouse. There won't be any problem getting a very quick court order after showing Judge Larsen surveillance still pictures that the FBI took outside that location a month ago."

Thorne almost came unglued.

"What do you mean 'pictures'? This is the first I've heard of them! What else is the FBI withholding?" he demanded.

"Calm down," James said. "I planned on showing you the surveillance pictures a short time ago, before the upcoming party would take place."

Shirley interrupted and explained, "A few weeks ago, Tom and Ted had referred to this subject. They said they had pictures outside of a farmhouse where they believed a shucking party had taken place. This was when Ted had told me what a shucking party involved. I was going to tell Jason about it after I reviewed the pictures, but I forgot to tell him because I hadn't actually seen them myself."

The buoyant, playful Greg of earlier in the day was gone, and was now replaced by an angry, aggressive attorney.

"I demand to know more about how my client will be protected if anything goes wrong at this shucking party. I need to know what this stupid thing actually is. And then my client and I will either agree to John's participation or not."

Thorne conceded that this was an understandable demand. Shirley suggested that she take John into her office until all the particulars were worked out, and they could fill her in afterward. Thorne agreed and moved toward the door as John pushed his chair back and stood up.

"Don't do anything that I wouldn't do," Greg whispered to him before he was escorted out of the room.

****

Shirley's office was just a few doors down from the conference room. The interior was strikingly similar to Thorne's office: plain and simple. John wondered if it was standard protocol, or if maybe the DA's budget just couldn't afford decent office furniture.

John sat across from Shirley at her desk, and to his surprise, she began asking him personal questions about Greg.

"Don't take him too seriously. He likes to project a certain image, but it's not really him," he said.

Shirley looked slightly put off by his description, so he scrambled to save it and offered, "He's a really great guy. A super friend!"

This time, she managed to produce a smile. She took out a business card and wrote her home number on the back of it.

"Give this to Greg," she said, and handed it to John.

****

Meanwhile, Thorne explained to Greg the kind of surveillance that would be used, as well provided a synopsis of what a shucking party entails. Greg told Jason that he did not want John to wear a wire. It would put John in a dangerous situation if they somehow realized his client was recording their conversations.

Jason agreed that the surveillance equipment would pick up everything they needed and John wouldn't have to wear a wire. Finally, Greg was convinced and he agreed to recommend to his client that he attend the shucking party.

Shirley and John returned to the conference room twenty minutes later and the meeting was adjourned.

On their way out, Greg passed Shirley and told her in a low, confident voice, "Next time, I want dessert! Dark chocolate is my favorite."

Shirley smiled back.

****

John and Greg left the building with a sense of accomplishment. They had achieved what they'd set out to do. Plus, Greg had scored a number. John hadn't seen his friend so happy as when he handed over Shirley's business card with her handwritten number on the back.

"I can't believe Shirley would pass on her number to a perv like you," John remarked.

"Stick with me, I'm on a roll, kid," Greg retorted.

"To be honest, I have a hard time even thinking about women with all of this shit I'm going through."

Greg smirked and looked at him skeptically.

"I bet you don't have any trouble thinking about that hot Filipino."

John looked away with disgust. Greg was the consummate horndog, without a doubt!

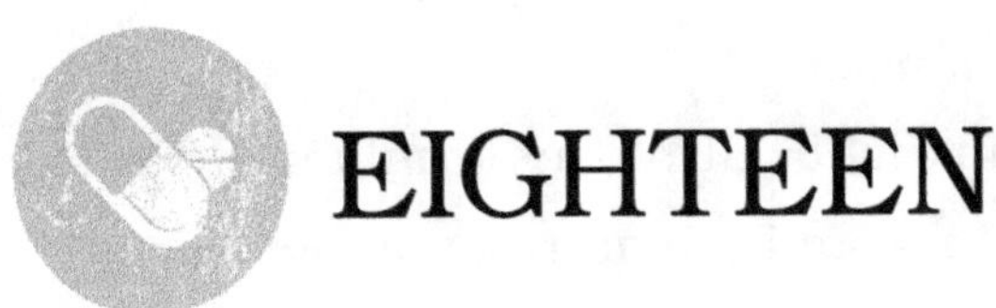 # EIGHTEEN

Before John knew it, Saturday had arrived, along with Ryan honking his Grand Prix in the driveway. They rode in silence all the way out to Chuck's farmhouse in rural Kansas, just south of Paola. John noticed that fifty yards adjacent to the white farmhouse with its limestone foundation was a matching old barn. He looked up to the sky and around the premises and wondered how close Tom James and Ted Bishop really were. Thorne and his merry group had succeeded in securing a court order so that they could set up surveillance equipment inside the farmhouse and outside the perimeter.

As John got out of Ryan's company car, he noticed the line of other Chalk Pharma company cars parked at the farmhouse. It was practically a convention. Aside from the cars, the gravel drive was empty. Everyone was already inside the rustic farmhouse. He went inside and imagined Quantrill's Raiders using the farmhouse as their hideout after they burned down Lawrence, Kansas.

Once inside, he noticed six card tables set up with a chair under each. At one table sat Joe Arnold, at another table was Mavis Turner, and to John's surprise, Mike Currey was seated at another.

What did they do to Mike to get him to join? John wondered.

Ryan arrived behind Mike's table and yelled, "Are you boys ready for some serious shucking?"

John wanted to run right out of the farmhouse. He still had no idea what was in store for him, nor was he completely confident that he could keep up the front that he was part of the group. He calmed his nerves by glancing around the room and reminding himself that there was surveillance equipment watching his every move.

For the first time after entering the farmhouse, John was intrigued when he noticed there was an old Western-style bar, complete with old style Western lamp lights and weathered, leather stools. It looked like a scene right out of *Gunsmoke*. Behind the bar, he noticed a black, wood-framed canvas depicting a gang of outlaws on horseback, with drawn pistols, leaving the scene of a bank robbery in the Old West. On the floor in front of the bar was an antique wooden crate on coasters, which had been filled with cubed ice.

"Here, buddy, sit down," Ryan said, and pulled out a chair for him at an empty card table next to Joe Arnold. John took the seat and Arnold slapped him on the back.

"You ready to earn some real money, rookie?" he exclaimed.

"Always!" John lied. "I've got a high-maintenance hen whom I've gotta keep happy."

"Bet that's some premium muff you're getting!" Arnold returned.

Ryan caught on to their conversation.

"Joe, enough with the triple-X material. We've got some serious things to discuss with John."

He gestured toward Mike, who was working at his table with a stone face. He had several boxes of drug samples in front of him that were from other pharmaceutical companies. In addition, he had a big straw basket to his left and a huge, aluminum garbage can with a plastic liner inside.

John noted his routine: He would take pharmaceutical samples, pop them out of their package, throw the pills into the basket, and then toss the empty cardboard boxes and aluminum packages into the garbage can.

The whole thing disgusted John. Not only was it illegal, but there was absolutely no hygienic care—no tablecloths, no sterile rubber gloves.

"You are now witnessing the art of shucking," Ryan proudly announced.

He then directed John's attention to Mavis Turner. Mavis had boxes and bottles of samples; however, he also had several boxes of cotton balls and bottles of acetone. He was picking up one capsule at a time and wiping off the embossed "sample" from each capsule with acetone on the cotton square. After that, Mavis would throw the capsule into a basket and discard the empty bottles and boxes into the trash can.

Ryan accompanied John to Joe's table and John noticed for the first time that Joe had several razor blades in front of him. He held one blade in his hand and a sample in the other and, after one motion, John saw that he was literally shaving off the imprinted "sample" before throwing them into the basket. John grimaced at the fact that Joe was completely altering the dosage of the pharmaceutical. On the table was a pile of shavings made entirely of discarded medicine.

"All right, now sit your ass down at your table," Ryan instructed. He may have been joking, but his voice had an edge to it.

"I've got to admit, this is one strange party," John confessed.

Ryan brought over several large, cardboard boxes with different types of drug samples in each one. He told John that his job was to separate the samples by type of drug. There were to be three piles of drug samples. Then he was to carry the samples to a bedroom located off of the living room and put each type of drug sample into their respective pile so the other three could go in and carry back an ample supply of that particular drug sample, which they were responsible for when they needed more.

"When you finish, bring your chair to my table and you can help me shuck Chalk Pharma's samples," Ryan said.

John saw stock bottles of Faxlot sitting at the fifth card table.

Ryan noticed John eyeing the fifty bottles and said, "It's hard to believe that there is over $20,000 in retail value sitting on that table alone, isn't it?"

"Where did it all come from?" John asked.

"I'm sure you're aware of the fact that pharmaceutical companies generally make stock bottles available to physicians on a limited basis when a drug is first introduced. Most of the time, these stock bottles are just kept in the sample closet with other samples. But one of the beauties of getting stock bottles is that their tablets are just like the ordinary retail tablets. In other words, the word "sample" isn't embossed or imprinted on the pill."

John shook his head and said, "Unbelievable." But he quickly overcame his shock and got to work. He didn't want to give the impression that he was opposed to what they were doing. After all, if they were capable of carrying out such an elaborate scam, what else could they do?

****

John kept reminding himself of the hidden surveillance devices. It was hard to believe that their every move was now being captured, bringing them one step closer to justice. He wondered if Tom James and Ted Bishop were parked nearby in a van, taking it all in. His thoughts were abruptly halted when the door to the farmhouse swung open and in stepped Chuck Frazier. The first person he saw was John and he walked right over and shook his hand.

"Glad to see you on such a beautiful Saturday afternoon," Chuck said. Then he went around and spoke with each participant in the shucking party. The man would have made an excellent politician. But John still couldn't believe how naïve he had been. It seemed like just a few days ago that he had viewed Chuck as his mentor. Now, he envisioned how Chuck would look behind bars with the rest of his shucking gang.

Finally, Chuck took his own card table. Ryan asked John to come over and help him with the Chalk Pharma samples and soon, he was emptying bottles of his own company's samples onto the table while Ryan shaved off the imprinted word "sample." John could see Chuck out of the corner of his eye, laboring over an open notebook, keeping tabs on the in- and outflow of meds.

Chuck rose from his chair and went outside. He returned after just a few minutes with two twelve packs of Bud Light and Coors, and a boom box under his arm. He set the boom box on the bar and unpacked the beer, placing the bottles in the ice crate.

He tuned the boom box to a country-western station.

"If any of you boys want to take a break, just go on up to the bar," he said.

Now it really was a party.

****

After drinking and shucking all afternoon, it was finally time to call it a day. All three of the drugs they had processed were now in large, plastic, dark-colored storage containers with lids. John wondered out loud if they had to put the drugs into containers or bottles before they left.

"Hell no!" Ryan responded. "That's FlatScott's job."

"You mean No-Ass will come out and count all those pills?" John asked.

"No, stupid," Ryan slurred. It was no wonder—he had put away quite a few Bud Lights. "Chuck will give them to FlatScott to count and rebottle with the help of his bottling and counting equipment," he said. "We shuck at least once a month, so get used to it!"

"I'm confused," John began. He saw Ryan bristle, but continued with his question anyway. "How are we getting our own samples for shucking?"

"We all order the maximum number of samples when the doctor signs on the computer for his samples, and we bring in less than what they had signed for. The extra samples are then kept by the rep and redirected to Chuck once a month. I'll show you how to do it the next time I work with you. Then you can contribute your preset amount each month."

"But what about other companies' pharmaceuticals?" John asked.

Ryan was exasperated, but he was also drunk and enjoyed the sound of his own voice, so he continued, "Real easily. The medical clinic staff doesn't take inventory of their sample closets. Without any inventory control, I can just look for the drugs we want and put them into my detail bag and exit the clinic with them. No questions asked. But never take all the samples of any particular drug. At the most, take only half of what they have on the shelf. That way, they'll never become wise as to what's actually happening."

Ryan gave him the whole rundown. He told John to always be careful when he took the samples out of his bag. No one should see him with them. The best bet was to wait until he got home, with his garage door down, before removing other companies' samples from the car. In this day and age, there was no telling when someone was watching from afar.

"I'll get you another detail bag next week," he finished. "That way, you can have two, just like everyone else."

****

Most of the drugs had been packed, and John was ready to go home. He headed out to the gravel driveway and saw Chuck closing his trunk. He wondered just how much money was now traveling in this man's car.

Chuck must have read John's mind because he said, "There's about a quarter-million to a half-million dollars' worth of pharmaceuticals that we separated today."

John's eyes must have grown to the size of saucers as Chuck segued to the fact that in the near future they would have a breakfast meeting.

"At this breakfast meeting, you'll get your share in cash for your hard work today."

****

As Ryan drove John back to his duplex, John thought about the money involved. If the gang was making $250K – $550K on samples each month, what kind of money could they be making from the third leg of the stool?

Diverting pharmaceuticals purchased directly from pharmaceutical companies at steep discounts for nursing homes and reselling them in the gray market had to be where the *real* big money came from.

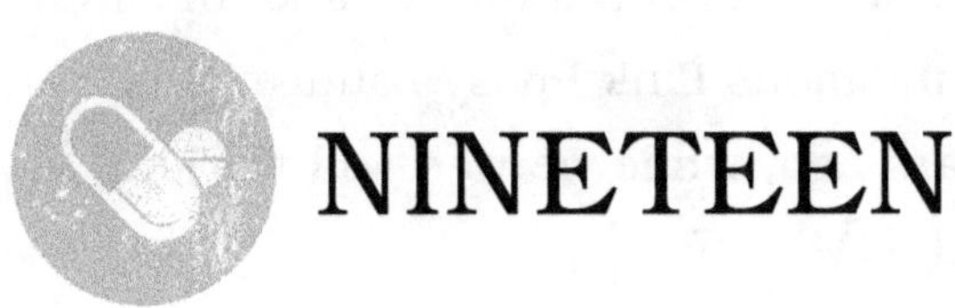# NINETEEN

ome once more, John went straight to his room and fell into bed. Just before hitting the mattress, he glanced at the clock: 7:00 p.m. Ryan Starr was a man of his word, after all, which made the whole ordeal of going undercover to his first shucking party seem even more surreal.

Before Ryan left, he'd reiterated, "Today's activities will pay big dividends from Chuck!" He had also said that in the very near future, he would give John a call so he could help FlatScott deal with some of his nursing-home situations.

John had forced a smile and said that he would be looking forward to it. But now that he was alone again and in a safe place, he regretted his choice of words. The party had worn him out and his fingers were sore from shucking the samples.

He had only long enough to observe the damage—a blister on his index finger—before he drifted off to sleep.

The phone woke him abruptly. *I can't even take a ten-minute nap!* John thought, but then he looked at the clock: 10:30 p.m. He'd been asleep for over three hours. He begrudgingly rolled out of bed and picked up the receiver.

"Why are you so shit-faced?" Greg exclaimed. It was an ironic statement, as his own speech was slurred and difficult to comprehend. But from what John could understand, his friend was at a titty bar—the infamous Pink Pussy Lounge. Greg had started going there years ago, while he was still working his summer internship at the DA's office.

"Is Shirley Phillips dancing there tonight?" John asked.

"She should be," Greg mumbled. "She's got better hooters, and a finer ass than any of these strippers."

John smiled.

"So, why are you calling?" he asked.

"Uh, duh—wondering how the sucking party turned out." Apparently this mistake was deliberate, as Greg started cracking up. When John didn't reply, he said, "Sorry, I meant *shucking* party. How was it?"

"Greg, you know I can't discuss it over the phone."

"I know, so bring your horny ass down here and let's have a good time!"

John looked at the clock again and figured, *What the hell.*

"I'll be there in fifteen minutes," he said.

"Hurry up! I've got Sally on my lap, and Molly's waiting for you."

John hung up, threw on some fresh clothes, and drove down to the Lounge. As he entered the strip club and paid the twenty-dollar cover charge, he couldn't help but ogle the waitresses. They were all dressed in pink outfits—if you could call a couple strips of cloth and fur an outfit. He spotted Greg two rows back from the main stage, sitting with a female stripper on each arm.

Greg saw him walking over and yelled out, "Milkman has arrived!" Then he turned to both dancers and introduced them as Sally and Molly.

"Aren't they beautiful?" Greg exclaimed.

They were not only beautiful, but they were identical twins. Greg reached into his shirt pocket and pulled out two crisp ten-dollar bills and gave one to each twin. "Come back in twenty. And send a pink waitress over," he said.

They stood up and, after landing a big kiss on Greg's respective cheeks, did exactly as instructed.

"See the kind of clout I have in here, buddy?" Greg bragged.

"I wasn't even aware that you so frequently patronized this place anymore," John replied.

"Can't tell you all of my secrets, now can I? Now down to business: How did that suck-shuck party turn out?" Greg asked.

But before John could answer, an attractive brunette waitress asked them if they wanted a round of shots.

"Another round of Finger-Me-Good shots?" she asked.

Apparently, this is what Greg had ordered before John arrived.

"Tell you what, sweetie. How about you get us two shots of Patrón and two Michelob Lights?"

The waitress nodded and headed off to fetch his order.

Finally, Greg sobered up a bit and for the first time, spoke without a slur.

"Now really, how did it go?"

John told him that it was one of the weirdest experiences of his life. "The whole afternoon, I kept wondering where the surveillance cameras were hidden and where Ted Bishop and Tom James were hiding."

"It's just as well that you didn't know." Greg said.

He was about to continue, but the waitress arrived with their drinks. John gave her a twenty-dollar tip and told her to just keep the tab running. *Honey.*

John told Greg about the mechanics of the shucking party and asked him how much he thought the pharmaceuticals were worth in retail. Greg guessed *in the ballpark of fifty grand.* When John told him the real answer, Greg's eyes nearly popped out of his skull.

"No shit!" he shouted.

Greg was so loud that the men surrounding their table all turned to look. John motioned with his hands for Greg to keep his voice down and then proceeded to tell him that there might be even more money in selling pharmaceuticals diverted from nursing homes to the gray marketplace.

"On the other hand," he said, "the $250,000 to $500,000 worth of drugs I saw today would be all profit because they hadn't spent a dime on any of it. They were all stolen samples from other companies, as well as our own."

John told Greg about what Ryan had said about the payout in the future, as well as more work that needed to be done with FlatScott at the nursing homes.

"Do you think we need to set up another meeting with Thorne's office?" he asked.

"I'll talk to Jason and make sure they've received everything they wanted from the surveillance equipment. I'll also let them know about what Ryan told you in the car. Jason can decide on whether or not we need to meet up."

Once they had concluded their conversation about the shucking party, Greg reverted back to his drunken state. John couldn't figure out if Greg was really drunk, or just a very good actor, but he had a feeling that it was somewhere in between.

John wasn't interested in seeing his friend get shit-faced, so he waited around for thirty minutes before announcing he had to leave. He wanted to get some sleep before meeting Sara the next day for church and lunch.

John stood up from the table, but quickly sat back down. He turned to Greg, who was calling to the brunette, but when Greg caught sight of John's face, he sobered up.

"What's wrong?" he asked.

John leaned forward and whispered two words: "Simple Simon."

He had just seen him entering the club with the same muscular nurse, except this time, she was dressed in black leather pants and a matching jacket. She looked completely different than she had before. Simple Simon looked exactly as he always did—like a hoodlum from the sixties. He wore a dress hat and trench coat, and a stern face to go with them.

Greg gave Simple Simon and his companion the once-over and asked, "Is that really him?"

John confirmed that it was and Greg told him that he had seen that wobbly old man and strange woman in the joint numerous times over the years. In fact, one of the waitresses had told him a few years back that the old man was the owner.

What happened next confirmed his story: Two of the bouncers walked over and shook Simple Simon's hand. The hot female bartenders even came out from around the bar to say hello.

Sally and Molly rejoined their table.

Greg casually asked, "Who's that old geezer that looks like he walked off the set of *The Godfather?*"

"Oh, that's the owner," Sally confirmed. Or maybe it was Molly. Greg couldn't tell; they were identical, after all.

"Who's the lady in the leather?" John asked.

Neither of them could say who she was, but they had heard that she was his live-in nurse and bodyguard. They'd also heard that she was a third-degree black belt in karate. At least that explained her stature. She certainly looked like an athlete in that tight, leather outfit. Even at a distance, those hands looked as big as catcher's mitts.

The bouncers escorted the pair to a table about fifteen yards from where they were sitting. As soon as they were seated, the DJ cut the music and asked that all dancers come to the stage. The twins left their side and joined the twenty-five other women on the stage and began to put on a special show. As they writhed to the music in their triangle tops and G-strings, John told Greg that he had to leave before the old man saw him.

"At the end of the song," Greg said. "The lights will dim again and it won't be so bright. Leave then."

John waited in agony for the song to end. He was poised and ready to make a clean escape when the waitress reappeared with a bottle of Dom Pérignon and four glasses. The twins joined them as the waitress said, "Compliments of Mr. Simon."

As the waitress said this, she handed John a folded piece of paper. He opened it and read the short message:

John,

Have a good time. Your waitress knows that the tab for

you and your companion is on the house.

The waitress popped the cork and champagne flowed out.

Without missing a beat, Sally said, "Greg, that reminds me of you."

"Shut up, Sally," Molly hissed. "Greg is mine!"

For a minute, John thought the twins were going to get in a catfight. Before it escalated even further, John leaned over and whispered that it was too late for him to run.

"I think you're right," Greg agreed. "Simon is staring at you right now. Acknowledge the champagne and note, man."

They both waved and nodded their heads at him. Simon tipped his hat back in reply. For the first time, John saw Simon's companion crack a smile.

Greg looked at John and said in a low voice, "This just keeps getting weirder and weirder, doesn't it?"

****

A few glasses of champagne later, Sally and Molly were getting anxious to earn some money and started pressuring them for a lap dance. Even Greg declined and told the girls that he and John needed to do some talking.

"Do the rounds, girls. Come back later."

As soon as the sisters moved on, John asked Greg why he thought Simon would want to own a place like this at his age.

"Are you kidding me?" Greg snorted. "The Pink Pussy Lounge is the perfect cover for mob activities. First of all, you have an easy setup for money laundering from other illicit operations. Secondly, the mob is involved with prostitution. Third, the mob is also involved in narcotics. All three converge in a place like this."

John looked around, blinking nervously.

"I wonder if any of that half-million will make it back into this club?"

"Who the fuck knows," Greg responded.

John happened to glance up at the stage and noticed that an extremely well-endowed Asian woman was showing her wares. Greg noticed too.

"It's incredible what people will do for money," he remarked.

John nodded in agreement. But the more he thought about it, the more he realized that his friend could just as easily have been speaking about him. After all, he was acting as a snitch not just for the valor, but also for the money he would receive from turning in his boss and coworkers. The thought depressed him.

"I'm taking off, man," John said. "Give me a call after you talk to Jason."

Greg nodded in agreement, but kept his eyes pinned on the show before him.

John stopped in the restroom before leaving. On his way out, he looked back at Greg's table and saw that the twins had returned. Molly was giving Greg a lap dance while Sally watched, fuming. Simple Simon had the same look on his face that John remembered from the coffee shop. His companion, however, was enjoying herself, taking swig after swig from her own, personal bottle of champagne.

****

John was relieved to stumble back into his own bed. He thought about how lucky he was to have a girl like Sara so that he didn't have to frequent a place like the Pink Pussy every week.

He briefly entertained thoughts of asking her to move in, but quickly threw that idea out the window when he reviewed his current situation. There was no way he could ask her to either live with or marry him while he was involved in uncovering illegal activities.

Life can be a real bitch, John thought as sleep found him once more.

# TWENTY

With each passing day, John grew increasingly more anxious about his undercover operation. It was difficult for him to enjoy a few moments alone with Sara, let alone get some work done on his own. But time did seem to fly by, pulling him closer to the day when he would see Ryan Starr again and learn more about their corrupt dealings.

The Tuesday after the shucking party, Starr made good on his offer to John and said he would get back to him about the logistics of seeing FlatScott soon. He said it was for some additional training—John would soon take over a couple of nursing-home accounts that had been his—but John knew there was more to it than that.

Ryan had decided to have them meet at RX Health, the very same place where John had first met FlatScott. When John arrived, Ryan was there, waiting for him. John had to admit that Ryan was always an *eager beaver.*

Starr led him to the back room where they found Chuck and FlatScott having coffee and donuts from Lamar's, another Kansas City staple. As soon as Chuck saw John, he ushered him over.

"John Boy, come in here and have some breakfast."

FlatScott stood up and shook his hand cordially and then gestured to the half-empty box of delicious doughnuts. John grabbed a custard-filled long john and hot cup of joe even though he would have preferred hot chocolate. He wondered what would come next.

Chuck was in an extremely good mood. His face positively shined as he handed a blue duffel bag over to John. John looked at it curiously.

"Open it," Chuck urged.

He set aside his doughnut and coffee and did as he was told. John unzipped the bag and his eyes grew wide. It was filled to the brim with greenbacks held together by thick rubber bands.

"There are various denominations of used bills in each stack," Chuck said.

John was in awe. He didn't know if it was polite, but he asked anyway, "How much does this all add up to?"

Chuck put his hand on John's shoulder and exchanged a glance with each man in the room.

"There's $40,000 worth of non-traceable greenbacks in that duffel bag. It's your share of the party."

John nearly dropped the bag. He was holding more money in one hand than ever before in his life. And it was all for him! His greed swelled and made him think for a moment that he shouldn't have cooperated with the government; continuous cash like this could set him up for life. The thought lasted only for a moment.

"That's a great deal of money!" John exclaimed, regaining his composure.

The men cracked up. Ryan laughed so hard he spilled coffee on his tie and suit pants.

"Does this mean you're happy with your share from the shucking party?" Chuck asked.

"Extremely," John answered. And he was, even if he was still torn by their illicit activities. He had never imagined such a quick—and hefty—return. "I can't believe you turned the drugs into money so quickly."

"We have our ways," Chuck replied.

"So what am I supposed to do with all of this cash?" John asked.

Ryan started laughing again; he had a hard time controlling himself, but the other men did not. Chuck shot a look at Ryan and he immediately clammed up.

"That's actually quite smart of you to ask," he said. "The best thing to do is hide the majority of it. Every week take $10,000 or so and divide it up among five or six banks and make deposits. Never put more than a couple thousand in one bank. You can write checks to pay off bills, invest it, or spend it."

Ryan said that he had some strong mutual funds that John might be interested in. But John had a lot of credit card bills that he wanted to pay off—and quickly—but politely turned him down. For a brief moment, John realized that he had forgotten the reality of the situation.

"Isn't it hell when you don't know what to do with all the loot?" FlatScott asked.

Chuck moved toward John and put his arm around him.

"We'll help you with the additional income in three months or so. We can even show you how to invest it in some of our enterprises. But we'll wait until you pay off some bills first."

John's gaze remained on the floor as he nodded his head in agreement. Chuck told him to always be careful with what he knows. There was no telling who might be listening to what he says.

"Don't forget to keep all this information confidential," he said, pointing his finger at John to emphasize the point. "This remains within our own little family."

Chuck stood up and reiterated his belief that John would do fine in their family.

"We always take care of family. Just like the dead-doctor issue," he said.

You framing asshole, John thought, but of course, he didn't betray his anger. Instead, he nodded his head again in gratitude.

"All right, gang. Time to meet up with Simple Simon and deliver his share for the month," Chuck announced, and headed out.

As soon as Chuck left, FlatScott headed up the discussion.

He stated to John, "RX Health supplies four nursing homes with their medications. A couple of these are exceptionally large nursing homes."

"Is that where a lot of the shucking samples are used?" John asked.

Ryan answered for FlatScott through his shit-eating grin.

"You really are bright. A bright dumbshit!"

FlatScott tried to smooth over this comment by saying, "No John, those pharmaceuticals do not play a role in the nursing homes. During your training, did you ever work for a pharmacy that dispensed to nursing homes?"

"No, can't say I've ever worked in that particular setting. Just hospitals and retail."

"Well, pharmacies that have contracts with nursing homes provide them with their pharmaceuticals on a daily basis. Plus, the pharmacy has to provide other services, including emergency assistance with medications. A pharmacist needs to be on call 24/7."

FlatScott wanted John to have this information because he knew John was a fellow pharmacist and they might need his expertise once a month on a Saturday or Sunday to help fill the nursing-home orders or a few scripts in the retail pharmacy. Also, if they got bogged down, then John could help them out after his Chalk Pharma day was over.

"As you know, the state pharmacy inspectors will be in this store, as well as our other four stores, periodically. We do all our nursing-home business out of this pharmacy. It's our main location. This will be the only store that I will ask you to work at every now and then."

John agreed to do the extra work, but he was confused about why the nursing-home enterprise was so profitable.

"Are all of the other reps in this district involved in the nursing homes?" he asked.

"No, it's actually just us three. Ryan's been a big help to me, in the same way that I hope you will be."

"Well, I'm happy to help in any way I can," John said. "I know that a few pharmacies have contracts with nursing homes, but I thought it was just income to help make a good living. I still don't see where these incredible profits could be generated."

Once again, Ryan interrupted with his idiotic laughter. But instead of ignoring him, John flipped him the bird.

FlatScott laughed at the antics of these two young men.

"Gentlemen, please. Let me answer John's question." He waited for quiet to resume before continuing. "We have contracts with pharmaceutical companies for their drugs to be used in nursing homes with deep discounts on those drugs."

John was confused.

"But I always thought that the contracts with the manufacturers for nursing homes and other institutions prohibited reselling the drugs."

FlatScott said that he was right: The contracts with the manufacturers always had a clause in them banning the resale of drugs.

"Do you mean we are defrauding the pharmaceutical companies?" John asked.

FlatScott looked at John and said, "That's exactly what I mean."

John found this news distressing, and FlatScott clearly noticed.

"John, I can tell you think we are crooks. But you know—and I know—that it's the pharmaceutical companies who are the crooks. In reality, the prices that we are getting for these drugs are what the pharmaceutical companies should be selling them for anyway."

"How deep are these special discounts?" John asked.

"It varies between 25 percent and 80 percent, depending on the pharmaceutical."

"Do you mean that we buy a lot of pharmaceuticals at these deep discounts and then only dispense a portion of them at the four nursing homes?"

"Correct," FlatScott responded.

Now John was really bewildered, but this time, he didn't even try to hide it.

"Do we use all the shucking pharmaceutical samples, and all the samples that we don't dispense at the nursing homes, for resale through the RX Health stores?"

Both men allowed for a long period of silence before Ryan couldn't keep his trap shut any longer.

"You are really catching on, rookie!"

"There's more to it than just selling those drugs through our pharmacies," FlatScott followed. "I might as well fill you in on the rest of our distribution chain."

He settled into a chair now, and pointed to another for John to sit in.

"The majority of the pharmaceuticals we ship to a couple of wholesalers in other parts of the country at much higher prices than we originally bought them for. Some of these pharmaceuticals were to be used at the nursing homes that we have contracts with. Of course, we don't have any money of our own tied up in the shucked samples. The wholesalers resell the drugs to pharmacies across the nation. Therefore, these drugs end up being dispensed through retail drugstores across the entire United States."

"No shit!" John exclaimed.

Ryan laughed again, adding, "Not only that rookie, but we have every facet of this operation down to a fine science! We order enough pharmaceuticals through normal channels, or reputable wholesalers, so it looks like we get our goods from there."

Now that it was all out in the open, John figured he could be a little nosier.

"What kind of money could you make in a month by diverting pharmaceuticals away from nursing homes?" he asked.

"Wow, you are one greedy rookie," FlatScott joked. "The time will come soon enough—after you put in some work and some time goes by. Then you'll know the answer to that question firsthand."

"Must be ridiculously high if I just received $40,000 in a duffel bag," John remarked.

Ryan clapped his hands together and said, "Speaking of your duffel bag, why don't you take it home now and work for Chalk Pharma today."

****

John clutched the blue bag as he exited the store. He felt uncomfortable putting it in the trunk, so he drove with it in the passenger's seat. He even strapped the seat belt around it.

After getting home, he poured the money onto his fancy bed. Once again, he thought about how if he didn't have to turn the money into Thorne, he could pay off some of his credit card debt. He could whisk Sara off to the Philippines and spend a week getting a tan on the beach . . . he could—*No!* he thought. *No more fantasies. It's as good as blood money. Plus, it would take me longer than a week to tan!*

With great self-control, he put the cash back in the bag and hid it under a pile of dirty laundry in the bathroom. The more out of sight it was, the less likely it would be that temptation would get the better of him.

On top of the pile was a pair of bikini panties he had taken off Sara the night before. That was one temptation to which he was willing to give in. He headed back to his bedroom and decided to give his lady a call.

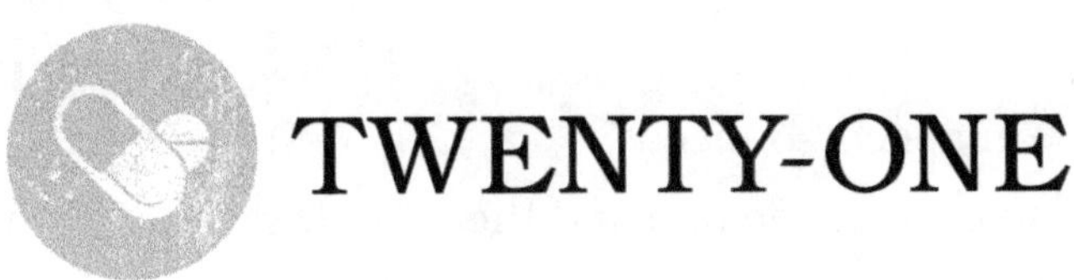 # TWENTY-ONE

After hearing about John's morning at RX Health, Greg called for an emergency rendezvous at the DA's office. He told John to hang tight while he got in touch with Jason. Immediately after hanging up with his friend, he had his new secretary connect him to Thorne's office.

The phone rang once, twice, three times—each ring carrying on until what seemed like the next century. Finally, the line was picked up. Greg prepared to greet the receptionist, but to his surprise, there was another, more familiar voice on the other end.

"Hey there, hot shot," Shirley Phillips cooed into the phone.

Greg wasn't sure why she was answering calls for the entire office, but after hearing her tone of voice, he was more than OK with the situation.

"Didn't expect to hear you on the other end," he said.

"The receptionist is sick today. I'm pulling double duty. If she's sick again tomorrow, Jason will have to hire a temp."

169

She spoke with a seductive softness—completely unlike her aggressive demeanor in the meetings. It was a voice that made Greg weak in the knees, and his mind raced to where he could take the conversation from there before it snapped back to the pressing matter at hand.

"Listen, sweetheart, can you please transfer me to Jason?" he asked.

"Well, since you asked so nicely."

Greg heard the click of the line and then a new greeting, but this time, instead of hearing Jason or Shirley, he was misdirected to one of the new attorneys in the office. Luckily, this attorney was capable of at least correctly transferring the call, and he finally heard Jason Thorne on the other end.

"What's going on?" Jason asked.

Greg told him about the discussion he'd just had with John, and Jason agreed that they should meet as soon as possible, but this time, he wanted it to be just the three of them.

"Let's go outside the office," he said, lowering his voice. "I want you to keep this confidential, but I think we might have a mole in the office. I have no idea who—that's the danger."

"What do you mean, 'a mole'?" Greg demanded. "How do you not know who it is?"

"I'll explain more at our meeting. Can't talk now."

He didn't even wait to say good-bye, and abruptly hung up.

As soon as Greg was off the call with Jason, his secretary transferred a call to him from Shirley.

She started talking immediately.

"I thought I'd hear from you after giving John my number to give to you."

"Dollface, you know I was planning on calling you. I just got tied up."

"Enough already. I'm sick of men beating around the bush. None of you have the balls to say what you really want, so I guess I'll have to be the one to do it. I want you. Saturday night. I'm going to a formal event, and if you're in after nine, I'll drop by with a couple bottles of booze and we can get to know each other better."

What Greg really wanted to do was yell, "You bet, baby!" but he knew that he had to play it cool. So he gave her his address and told her he was looking forward to Saturday night.

They said good-bye, and Greg realized that he might have just put himself in a compromising position. After all, Shirley was working on the case with him. But nothing had happened—yet. Greg decided that he would keep their Saturday plans to himself. Maybe he would tell John about it later, depending on what happened.

****

Later on, Greg received a fax from Thorne: *Let's have our powwow at Union Station tomorrow night. 7:00 p.m.*

Greg knew that he couldn't respond to Thorne directly; it was too risky, and so he just planned on bringing John with him to the meeting the next evening. Until then, he could only guess at what Jason would have to say about the snitch in the office.

****

It was all John could do to wait by the phone for Greg's call. While he was waiting to hear from him, he received a call from his comrade, Ryan Starr. Ryan invited him to a barbecue at Chuck's farmhouse on Saturday night. Dates were welcome and the party would start at seven thirty, but he wasn't to bring any food because Chalk Pharma was providing eats and entertainment for the night, as it was Chalk Pharma's annual summer picnic. John assured him that he would be there with his lady.

Fifteen minutes after he hung up, the call from Greg came in. Greg brought him up to speed on his conversation with Jason and gave him details on the meeting that was to take place the next night. However, Greg left out a crucial part. He did not tell John *why* Jason wanted to meet at Union Station. John had enough on his plate, and Greg was afraid that one more straw would be the one to break the camel's back. Luckily, John didn't even question why they were meeting at Union Station instead of Thorne's office—further proof that he was stressed and distracted.

"Hey, buddy, sorry to cut this short, but I've got to go. Got an appointment at a clinic in twenty minutes," John said.

"No worries, man. Talk soon."

Greg hung up and looked at the clock. It was five o'clock, which meant his receptionist would have left for the day. Just as this occurred to him, the phone rang. He picked it up and heard Ann Frazier's airy "Hello?"

The stud strikes again, Greg thought. First, he lines up a late-night rendezvous with Shirley, and now Ann was calling him. Hook, line, and sinker.

"I'd like to see you, Greg," Ann said. She paused for a moment before adding, "In a nonprofessional manner. I need some personal support, and I just don't know whom else I could talk to. All of my friends are connected to *him.*"

She was referring, of course, to her evil husband.

"Can we do your apartment, Friday night?"

Greg was caught off guard, and then said, "Meet me at my garage at eight o'clock and you know where I live."

She agreed, and sounded very relieved to have made plans for Friday.

Once he hung up with Ann, Greg finally let out his excitement and yelled, "What a day!"

It was the kind of day that called for brandy, which is exactly what he went to get.

****

On the way to Union Station, John saw that he had missed a call on his cell phone. He entered his voicemail passcode and once again heard Ryan's voice. *"Hey, rookie, Chuck wants you to know that it's a strict no-kids policy at this picnic. Chuck's serving spirits, and it doesn't sit well to have the innocents around while the adults are at play. Sunday-school teacher and his good, old-fashioned values, go figure."*

John hung up, wondering if he would ever be able to go an evening without having to take a message from Ryan Starr. He just couldn't seem to escape him. An eerie feeling came over John as he realized that practically every time he was to meet with Thorne, Ryan was trying to reach him to invite him out and draw him further into their drug-diversion scam.

The thought dissolved as he entered Union Station. He quickly spotted Greg motioning to him. Thorne had not yet arrived. John caught up with his friend, who looked extremely excited to have gained his company.

"Sit down. I have something to tell you."

John's face went blank. Normally, he wasn't so easily scared, but after the events of the past couple of weeks, John knew that "something" could truly be anything—good or bad.

"The reason why we are meeting at this location is because Jason thinks there is a mole in his office."

It wasn't as bad as John had expected, but still it confused and worried him. Before they could discuss it any further, Jason Thorne came walking briskly toward them.

They exchanged handshakes and then Jason took a moment to look around the station. It was a beautiful venue and looked unchanged since it was built in 1914.

"Let me share a little bit of Union Station history with you," Jason said, adding that he was a history buff and had even majored in the subject in college. "Seventy years ago this coming Saturday, the Union Station Massacre occurred. That was June 17, 1933. It lasted about a minute and a half. But in those precious moments, four law officials were killed, and a couple others were wounded. I'm sure you've both heard of the St. Valentine's Day Massacre in Chicago."

John and Greg nodded, wondering where this was going.

"The Union Station Massacre was even more meaningful when it came to the nation really wanting and supporting strong measures against crime. That's why I thought it only appropriate that we meet here: to remind us how serious this endeavor is. We should always remember the grave consequences, should we not take the utmost precaution."

Jason took another moment to gaze at the station and the people milling about.

"Anyway, if you want to learn more about the history of this place, Tom James and Ted Bishop enjoy talking about it just as much as I do, plus, I think they might even know more."

"So what's this have to do with the snitch?" Greg rudely interjected.

Jason turned to John and asked if he had heard about his suspicion that there was a mole in the office.

After listening to Jason's speech, in addition to this most recent update, John was more distraught than ever and managed to utter only "Yes."

"So why do you think there's a mole in the office?" Greg asked.

"Well, first, we never did know how Beth Beacon was found out. I've always suspected the possibility of a mole because of another investigation we were involved with. I became suspicious while I was working on another case concerning mob activities. It seemed like every lead we would get, every breakthrough, would get us nowhere. These guys were always two steps ahead of us. Even when the information we were acting on was highly classified. I could only conclude that someone had been tipping them off. Hopefully, I can find the parasite before he—or she—derails our efforts."

The odds of finding a mole in an office such as his were against him. These matters took time, but unfortunately they did not have a whole lot of time. Greg thought that maybe the mole was in the regional FBI office or the DEA. Jason thought it was possible, but because of some of the info that had been leaked, he believed it was in his own office.

John remained on the sidelines throughout the conversation, trying to process this new information. Finally, Jason asked him if there was any way he could work with FlatScott at RX Health in order to learn more information.

"I guess so," John agreed. "I might even have an opportunity to work with him sometime on an upcoming weekend."

"The sooner the better," Jason replied.

At this point, they had nothing with which they could prosecute Simple Simon. However, they believed that eventually, they would have plenty with which to go after Chuck and his cronies because of the PDMA guidelines.

"We need your eyes and ears open while you are working around FlatScott. If you can, take a look at some files to see if Simple Simon and Chuck have signed any incriminating documents," Jason said.

"I bet that Simple Simon hasn't signed a damn thing. Chuck, either," Greg replied.

"Nevertheless, we need our own mole working beside FlatScott to try to find out more about what's really going on."

John finally managed to calm himself down enough to speak with an even voice.

"I'll call FlatScott right away and see if they need me to report to work on Saturday."

"It seems we have an understanding," Jason remarked. "If you need anything, or if you find anything out, contact me immediately."

Greg couldn't let him leave on his own terms. Reasserting his authority, he told Jason to sit back down. Throwing his hands up in a mocking way, he sat down.

"Do you mean that you do not have proof on these SOBs for income-tax evasion yet?" Greg asked.

Jason squirmed in his seat and pointed out that this group was so good at laundering money through their other businesses—even a strip club—that there was no evidence that they could use to nail them on income-tax evasion. Somehow, the big money that was being made was constantly reinvested in illegal, as well as legitimate, enterprises.

"What about the bag of money I received? I'm sure others received their own bag too," John said.

"That money was laundered better than my perfectly pressed shirts," Jason replied.

"That reminds me. What should I do with the bag of money?"

"I must be getting old; I forgot all about it!" Jason exclaimed. "Of course, we eventually want it from you. Unless it makes you nervous, keep it for now. That way, if they ask you to invest in anything legal or illegal, you can give part of it back to them and we will know one more piece of the puzzle."

John claimed that he would hide it even better.

Jason smiled and said, "I'd caution you not to become too cavalier about it all. Some people would kill to get their hands on that amount of cash."

"Why don't you put it in a safe-deposit box?" Greg suggested.

Jason agreed with Greg's suggestion, and John said he would do it right away. Or maybe he would keep it in the duplex, just to look at. This last idea, John kept to himself.

Now that the money issue had been settled, Jason took off and left Greg and John alone to plot their next course of action. "What the hell have I gotten myself into?" John asked.

"Do you still have your Westerns-Style Coach Gun?"
John nodded.

"But I haven't fired it since we were teenagers. I remember it really destroyed that barn door."

"I still have my reproductions of the Walker Colt."

"Did you ever think we'd be the modern-day Wyatt Earp and Doc Holliday?" John asked.

John was joking with his comment, but for once, Greg remained serious.

"I'm going to put one of my Colts in the glove box of my car, and the other under my bed, loaded and ready."

"Yeah, I'll keep mine locked and loaded, and ready to blow someone straight to hell," John agreed.

Greg mused that they would definitely be breaking a few laws. "But at that point," he said, "who gives a fuck."

# TWENTY-TWO

The next morning, John called FlatScott and asked if he needed any help working at the pharmacy on Saturday. FlatScott told him that he was going to be at the picnic Saturday night, but if John could work Saturday morning, it would give him time to do other things besides filling orders.

"Report for work at eight o'clock Saturday morning," he said. John agreed and hung up.

His second call was to Greg to let him know he was going to work Saturday morning for FlatScott. He thought the call would be short and sweet, but they got caught up in a discussion about guns. Their conversation the night before had really gotten the wheels turning in Greg's head about protecting himself. Before John got off the phone, they agreed to check out some new pistols together and try them out at the local shooting range.

The next call he made was to Sara to invite her out to the picnic on Saturday night. Unfortunately, she was scheduled to work that evening, but she said she'd check with her supervisor to see if she could get the night off.

"Well, what about this evening?" he asked. "Would you like to join me for dinner and romance?"

"I thought you'd never ask," she said in a low, soft voice. "The answer is 'of course'!"

****

It was a slow day at the office, made even more painful by the fact that Greg could not stop thinking about Shirley Phillips. Finally, he gave in and called the DA's office. But to his great displeasure, a temp receptionist answered the phone. On top of that, Jason was not available to take Greg's call, so he decided to leave a carefully worded message.

"Don't put me through to voicemail. I want you to write this down and give it to him. Tell him that I called to let him know that the Milkman would be delivering the dairy as they had hoped on Saturday morning."

After getting off the phone, Greg decided he couldn't focus on work anyway and left to gather supplies for the weekend. He drove over to the pharmacy and picked up a new supply of condoms. As he walked down the aisle, he felt like a teenager shopping for his first rubbers. He decided upon a premium box that boasted, "Extra ribbed—for her pleasure!" He figured Shirley would like that. Before he left the aisle, he also grabbed a bottle of K-Y Jelly, just in case he needed it over the next two nights.

After this much-needed interlude, Greg returned to the office, only to be informed that he had missed a few calls. The most important one was from Jason, who let him know that he'd understood Greg's encrypted message.

His thoughts still on the weekend, Greg called his maid service to see if they could clean his apartment earlier than usual. Luckily, they agreed to come the next morning. Greg made a mental note to move the Colt he had hidden under his bed to his car, and then bring it back to the apartment later. The last thing Greg wanted was a maid wondering why he had a loaded gun stashed in his room.

****

That evening Sara rang John's doorbell and upon answering the door, she smelled his world-renowned lasagna (as John called it). Conversely, John took in the sight of a woman whose looks trumped even the most delicious heavenly goods.

Sara was delighted by the candlelit dinner that John had arranged, and it quickly crossed her mind that tonight might be the night that he popped the question. Sara knew in her heart that her answer would be yes, but upon hearing John's voice as he asked her to sit down, she realized that John was a practical man and it was far too early in their relationship to make such an irrational leap.

The two sat down to their Italian meal, which included a fine bottle of Chianti. They chatted about work—or rather, Sara told him about happenings at the hospital. The last thing John wanted to talk about was work, so instead, he asked her if she was able to get Saturday night off.

"I asked, but no word yet," she replied.

"Well, if you go, bring your pom-poms. The guys and I are going to play some pickup basketball, and I'm going to need all the moral support I can get—especially if I go up against Mavis. The man's like a foot taller than me!"

Sara laughed and said she'd love to be his cheerleader.

After dinner, instead of playing romantic music and cuddling on the couch, John turned on the TV set and switched the channel to an NBA Finals game.

Sara rolled her eyes at John, who had moved to his oversized recliner. *Tonight is definitely not the night,* she lamented. She stretched out on the couch, all alone on such a big piece of furniture.

"Hey, buddy, why don't you come over and keep a girl company?" she yelled.

Once John managed to peel his eyes away from the TV set, he realized his blunder. He apologized and walked over to join her. He started talking about the game, and how there was a Drake player he wanted to check out. This talk about basketball continued for some time, although Sara stopped listening fairly early on. Instead, she thought about how he would probably love to give her a basketball, but there was no way in hell he was going to give her a ring anytime soon.

But then he surprised her. During the second half of the game, and second bottle of Chianti, John started to talk seriously about their future. He told her that he loved her and would one day ask her to be his wife. He even talked about a family with her: three kids, all the best-looking ones in their class because of their mixed heritage. Such serious talk pulled him from the game, and both of them into the bedroom.

****

As they lay in bed together, naked and cooling off on top of the sheets, John realized that he couldn't keep his secret from her any longer. If this was a woman he planned to stay with until the end, then she had to know everything. So he asked her to rest her head on his chest and spilled the story to her, every sordid detail.

He thought Sara was going to pass out when he told her about going to Jason Thorne's office. Her reaction made him decide not to show Sara the money that was now hidden under his bed. On the other hand, it turned him on to think about the $40,000 under his bed, with Sara on top. But when he saw Sara crying because she was worried about his safety, he realized he needed to comfort her. Trying to get a laugh, he changed the subject.

"I don't know what Greg is up to in his personal life, but I'm sure there's a dirty-legged slut involved," he said.

"What the hell does that mean?" she asked.

John responded, "You know!"

"I don't know!" she replied, and the two burst into laughter.

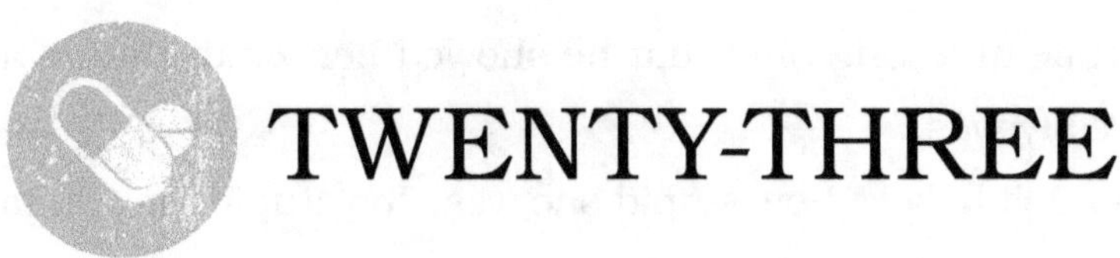# TWENTY-THREE

Sara left during the night, and it took John a moment to remember why he was alone when he woke up. As he thought back on their evening together, he felt relieved that she was finally privy to what was going on. However, he realized that he had neglected to tell her about the very large amount of money he would receive if this whole mess turned out the way they hoped.

He thought about how, with that kind of money, Sara and their future family would have a head start on life. On the other hand, he thought that maybe it was just as well she didn't know about the financial end of the game. John was wary of Sara thinking he was motivated strictly by money and materialism.

****

Chuck Frazier could not believe his marriage was in the shitter. The day before, his wife had come to him in tears and informed him outright that she wanted a divorce. The final blow came when she told him that she had, in fact, already been to see an attorney. Chuck had no regrets about slapping her right across the face for thinking she could pull such a maneuver.

After he hit her, he walked to the medicine cabinet and took the blue pill. When he went back to the room, she was still lying on the bed where she had fallen from the impact. He waited the necessary amount of time and then had his way with her. It was the first time in a long time that he showed her what kind of a man he really was.

He couldn't believe how stupid she was. Too stupid for him to even say, "You bitch, you signed a prenup, and won't get a dime from me." It was her assets that she had to worry about. And if she brought it up, he was ready to slam her down by telling her he didn't want her assets. He just married her for her tight little ass.

Ann slept in one of the spare bedrooms after he was done. He was left alone to watch basketball and fall asleep, trying to remember which subject he would be teaching to his Sunday school class that weekend. He had been so busy thinking about all that had transpired over the course of the last day that he didn't even realize the weather outside was phenomenal. It was the perfect summer day in Kansas City, and once he realized this, that gave him hope for his planned outside activities at the picnic Saturday evening.

****

Chuck pulled up the long, steep driveway to Simple Simon's house. By this time, he was feeling like a real man and strutted to the back door to ring the doorbell.

Belle answered the door. Chuck grinned, not because he was happy to see her, but because he had guessed how she would be dressed. For some reason, Belle loved to wear jumpsuits. It was one of those suits with the zipper in front from the neckline all the way down to her crotch.

Chuck could not help but think he should have been an ob-gyn. However, he knew he was thinking in a perverted way because of that bitch wife of his.

This morning, Belle's color of choice was navy blue and the zipper was pulled down to show a little cleavage, as usual.

"Chuck, have a seat at the kitchen table. Simon just woke up and will be with you shortly," Belle bellowed.

Chuck helped himself to a mimosa he made from ingredients in the fridge. He liked the idea of having a drink because the previous day had been so trying. He also helped himself to scrambled eggs, bacon, and whole-wheat toast, which were all set out in insulated foil containers on the counter. Chuck realized that there was a lot of food in the containers. He had thought that the meeting would be just the two of them—three, with Belle. But it certainly did not seem that way.

****

Belle went into the master bedroom and walked all the way back to the bathroom, where Simple Simon was seated in the Jacuzzi to relieve the pain of his old, tired body. He had been in the hospital for a few days with kidney stones, and the week before, he had been admitted to the hospital for a couple days with acute gastritis due to excessive alcohol consumption. He was even more on edge than usual.

"Where were you?" he snapped. "I've been waiting for you to scrub my back."

Belle looked at him pityingly and asked, "Oh, did my S.S. get up in a bad mood?"

Simon gave her a dirty look. He hated her nickname for him. Heinrich Himmler's Waffen SS had killed his parents in World War II. Belle thought it funny to call him that name when he acted rudely toward her. It was her own little joke on one of the most feared men in Kansas City, if not the whole country.

"Anyway, Chuck Frazier is waiting for you in the kitchen. Probably pigging out on bacon and booze as we speak," Belle said.

Simple Simon waved her away and went back to resting in the tub, but Belle wouldn't leave.

"Did you have fun with that kiddie hooker at the club last night?" she asked.

"Fuck off," he replied. He stood up as quickly as he could and grabbed the bath towel.

"Your clothes are laid out for you on the bed," Belle said, and disappeared back into the kitchen.

She made it downstairs just in time to hear a knock on the door that led to the basement. Belle proceeded to unlock the door. Two men came in through the doorway and went directly to the breakfast buffet. Like Chuck, they had done this routine many times.

When Belle came over with two freshly made mimosas, one of the men said, "I don't drink pussy-willow drinks."

"I apologize," she said. "I have many things on my mind and forgot your preference." She took a mimosa away and returned with a cup of strong, black coffee and a shot of whiskey on the side.

Chuck broke the silence among them and said that maybe he should consider moving to the neighborhood. That way, he'd have access to the tunnel so he could also arrive through the basement, undetected. The comment did nothing to break the ice, and the two men just stared at Chuck, the outsider. Thankfully, Simon arrived and they all stood up to shake hands.

"When you're all finished with breakfast," he said, "bring your fat asses into the den."

"Would you like the usual? Boiled egg and coffee?" Belle asked.

Simon snapped at her, "You can stick that egg up your ass. I'm not hungry now."

The men broke out in laughter, but a sideways glance from Simple Simon shut them all up. Belle could care less what those men thought of her. She knew she was an accomplished nurse, and with her black belt, she could kick any of their asses, no matter how fat.

****

The meeting between Simple Simon, his two capos, and Chuck lasted for almost three hours. As the men spoke, Belle periodically came in and out with drinks and snacks for the men, catching snippets of their conversation here and there.

At one point, she walked in to hear Simon say, "Belle will handle that situation," but didn't know what it applied to. She did know, however, that in the near future, Simple Simon would be giving her some new marching orders.

She then heard Simon ask the capos whether or not they had bought the new guns that could be loaded as a pistol or a shotgun.

"Everybody in our crew has one," one of the capos scoffed.

Simon was delighted that his group was outfitted with a weapon that had lots of flexibility.

Later, after bringing another round of coffee and whiskey for the group, she heard one of the capos saying there had to be a way to save their business because it was worth millions. Chuck nodded his head in agreement and asked, "Are you sure that FlatScott has to be eliminated?"

She couldn't hear Simon's answer.

Upon returning to clear more plates, cups and glasses, she heard Simon continue his scolding.

"Chuck, you and your people are not as good as you think. Our mole in the DA's office has informed me that they have incriminating evidence on you. However, the mole has been able to destroy the recordings that illustrate your stupidity for talking to Ryan about various shit over the phone," said Simon.

Chuck was in disbelief. Very few men were allowed to speak to him this way, and it was difficult to take.

Simon continued, "Our mole did what Dick Nixon should have done, and destroyed the recordings."

"Simon saved your bacon. Again," one of the capos retorted.

Chuck raised his glass and said, "Amen."

"There were other mistakes you made in this whole mess, besides us having to destroy the recordings to protect your ass. Because I was in the hospital, our mole was delayed in telling me about this John fucker supplying information to the DA's office. If I had received the information sooner, then we would have told you not to involve John. That way, we could have avoided this clusterfuck completely."

Chuck buried his head in his hands as he listened to Simon.

For some reason, Simon softened and said, "Don't put all the blame on yourself for this mess. At least we found out about it in time for us to take out all the surveillance equipment on the farm before the last shucking party."

At this point, Belle had leaned against the partially open door to listen in without them knowing she was there. She overheard Simon tell the capos that they had heard Chuck's personal problem and they might as well take care of it at the same time. From all of these snippets, Belle knew that Simple Simon would be handing out directives to be followed by his capos. Chuck would be involved too.

The meeting broke up and Belle could tell by the crashing noise down the stairs that one of the capos had drunk a little too much whiskey.

****

That afternoon, John received yet another call from Ryan. This time, it was about a change in Saturday night's plans. Ryan explained that Chuck had decided to bring in a speaker to talk to the reps about the new anti-inflammatory drug that had just come out. The speaker was going to be FlatScott. Therefore, the gathering on Saturday night was going to be stag—guys only!

"Don't worry, buddy. You can make it up to your girl later. Chuck said that the Christmas party will be extra special for everyone this year."

"Don't worry about it," John said. "My girlfriend just called a few minutes ago and she can't get off work anyway."

"Then it all works out," Ryan replied.

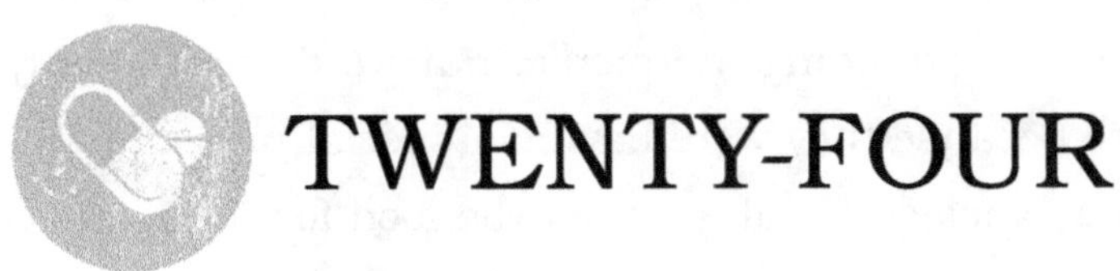# TWENTY-FOUR

Ann wasn't sure what had gotten into her. She hated her husband and desperately wanted to leave him, but running into the arms of another man? She tried not to think too much about it as she made her way to Greg's apartment on Ward Parkway.

Growing up, she had always thought her life would turn out to be perfect, and for a short time, it had seemed that way. She had married the perfect man, lived in the perfect house, and driven the perfect car. But as time went by, she realized that it was all a mirage—a disguise for something that wasn't actually there. And she just couldn't handle it anymore.

Chuck had tried to make it up to her earlier that evening by presenting her with a two-and-a-half-carat diamond necklace encased in white gold. He insisted on fastening it around her neck, and then kissed her on the cheek. She winced; it was the cheek he had struck the night before.

He patted her on her behind and said softly, "That's nice, baby."

Ann went to the mirror afterward and looked at her reflection for a good, long time until her rage had subsided.

Before she left that night, he handed her a list of items he wanted to be purchased for the picnic the following night. He told her she would be attending the picnic, but would be the only woman there because they were having a special presentation. She would be expected to take care of the food for the group— except for the barbecue, which he would do himself, of course. Once he had finished listing his demands, he headed towards his office, which was located on the first floor of their home.

Ann could hardly control her hatred for him and mumbled under her breath, "You worthless, fat-ass piece of shit."

****

She pulled into Greg's garage and quickly checked her makeup in the mirror to ensure her injured cheek and lip were properly camouflaged. She took out a tube of lipstick and used it to give her face a youthful flush. Finally, she stepped out of the car, ready for an encounter with a young man who she actually cared about.

She didn't have to walk very far before she spotted Greg's wiry frame waving to her from his driveway in front of his garage which he had made his way to. As soon as she saw him eagerly waving, she began to sob.

"What's wrong?" Greg asked and wrapped his arms around her.

"I'll tell you about it inside," she whispered, and the two walked very quickly toward his apartment.

Greg was behind her as they climbed the stairs to his domicile. He felt slightly guilty for watching her walk, but at the same time, he felt it was natural. The woman had one of the most sumptuous backsides he had ever had the pleasure of ogling.

Ann pulled out a paper sack once they entered his apartment. Inside was a fine bottle of Taittinger champagne, along with the diamond necklace in its case. Greg brought out a champagne bucket and filled it with ice. They then proceeded to the living room and sat on the couch. Greg placed two champagne glasses on coasters on the coffee table, and Ann put the necklace case beside the two glasses.

Greg kept telling himself they had to have some small talk and champagne before they got it on. He knew he had to take it slow. He thought of things they could talk about, but before speaking, Ann started the conversation.

She told him everything that had happened between her and Chuck over the past twenty-four hours. Everything, that is, except the part about Chuck raping her. She left that out because she wasn't sure what Greg's reaction would be, not to mention that it was embarrassing for her. However, she did tell him about Chuck smacking her.

Greg quietly listened. After hearing the part about Chuck hitting her, Greg stood up and walked down the hall. He came back carrying a wet washcloth and small hand towel and washed Ann's face. He gently dabbed at her makeup, her lipstick—everything that adorned this woman's beautiful face until he could see the vicious, purple bruises that streaked her cheek.

"That motherfucker!" Greg yelled.

Ann began to cry and they embraced. For the first time ever, Greg had discovered deep feelings for a beautiful woman, and he silently vowed to never let any harm come to her again.

Once Ann recovered, she reached for the necklace case and placed it in Greg's hands. He opened it and looked back at her, bewildered. Inside there was a note. He took it out and read it: *"Wear this 24/7. Love, Chuck."*

"He gave it to me a few hours ago," she said.

"Unbelievable," Greg replied.

"What do you think of what I just told you?"

"The only thing that I can make out from the whole story is that you married a violent psycho."

It was exactly what Ann needed to hear. She held his face and passionately kissed him. But when Greg's hands went up to cup her breasts, she pushed him away.

"I don't want you to think that I'm just some mixed-up, easy score for you," she said.

"In that case," Greg casually replied, "let's just have some more champagne and talk."

He told Ann that John had mentioned a couple of Chuck's friends who seemed like unique characters. He asked if she had ever heard Chuck comment on either Simon or Belle. Finally, for the first time that evening, Ann flashed a big smile that showed off her bright, gleaming-white teeth.

"I've met them both, and I can understand why John would mention them," she said.

Before she could go on, Greg asked, "Has Chuck ever commented on the relationship between the two?"

Ann thought about it for a moment.

"Well, it's certainly nothing sexual," she said. "The two of them have been together for a long time. Besides, Belle cares for Simon, and he gets enough action in the VIP lounge and back room at the Pink Pussy. Simon has always seemed to take great pride in getting along well with strippers."

Greg was surprised to learn that their relationship was platonic. It certainly didn't seem so at the club. Then he thought about Simon having fun with the strippers and realized that he had probably slept with some of the same girls as Simon. Greg had to laugh at the thought of it being such a small world that he'd shared the same stripper as a notorious, old gangster.

"If you think that story is funny, wait until you hear more," she continued. "Rumor has it that Belle hooks up with the bouncers all the time, sometimes more than one at a time. I've also heard that she's bisexual and was caught having sex with one of the female strippers!"

They both cracked up and gulped down more champagne.

"These are some majorly screwed up people we are talking about," Greg laughed.

Once again, Ann blindsided him and moved in for a passionate French kiss. *Is it the Taittinger or the sexy story?* he wondered. He wanted to store that strategy away for future use. This time, Ann didn't stop him from fondling her breasts, and before they knew it, they were between Greg's sheets.

****

Ann woke up first and saw that it was already ten thirty at night. She immediately got up from the bed and cleaned up, reapplying a fresh coat of makeup and lipstick. When she entered the hallway, Greg was waiting for her in a pair of old cut-off shorts. He walked Ann to the garage and kissed her good-bye.

Once she was in the car and on her way home, it suddenly dawned on Ann that she'd just had the best sex of her life. But now, with a sense of sudden terror, she realized she would have to get up in the morning before Chuck to shop for the items for his stupid party. She'd have to tell him that she had lost the receipt for the items in order to uphold the story that she had been out shopping for supplies, when in all actuality, she had been getting intimate with the very man who would be her divorce lawyer!

She knew receipts didn't matter anyway. Her husband would say, "Don't worry about it, I'll find a way to put it on the expense report." That's what he always did. Once again, it hit her that she was married to a crook.

Ann pulled into the garage, but before getting out of the car, she put on the diamond necklace. If Chuck wanted to play games, she could too. After her sexually charged night, the pendulum had definitely swung back to her side.

****

Before Greg fell asleep, he changed the sheets and pillowcases. He remembered a college roommate telling him that women could sense when another woman had been around from a mile away. Shirley was a sharp lady, and he didn't want her to think anything was amiss when he had her at his pad the following night.

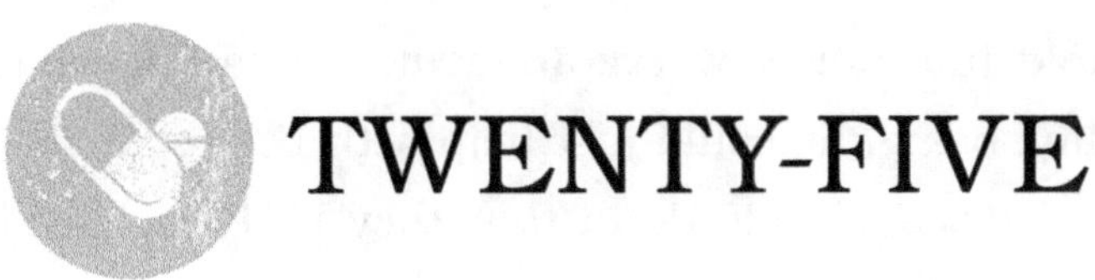# TWENTY-FIVE

John awoke early on Saturday to prepare for his big day of work at the pharmacy with FlatScott. He was slightly nervous on his drive over to the store, but the nerves were completely unrelated to his undercover work. These butterflies were due to his realization that he had never worked with nursing-home pharmaceuticals and he had no idea what duties FlatScott would have him do.

He went around to the back door and rang the bell. A very plump, dark-haired woman in her late forties unlocked the door. She seemed pleased to see him and stuck out her hand.

"You must be John," she said. "I'm FlatScott's wife, Jill. My friends call me 'Jelly.'"

What a couple they make, John thought, *FlatScott and Jelly! I wonder what the kids are named?*

"I've heard so much about you," she said. "It's about time we get some quality help at the store!"

As they walked in, she affixed her name tag to her shirt. It read "Jelly" and also declared that she was a pharmacist.

FlatScott popped into the room and extended his hand to John.

"I hope you remember I've never really filled orders for nursing homes," John cautioned.

FlatScott told him not to worry about it. He had decided that, for the time being, he could just help with the retail side of dispensing meds. Jelly told John that they had discussed it, and she would spend the day working on the nursing-home medications, and FlatScott would jump back and forth wherever he was needed.

John was relieved to not be working on the nursing-home side of the business. On the other hand, he realized that in order to achieve the goal of finding out more about that end of the business for Jason, he needed to get involved with it soon. John had to admit that he was glad that FlatScott and his wife decided not to put him in that area immediately. There would be plenty of time down the road to work and learn the secrets of that part of the business.

****

After a short warm-up period, John actually found it fun to be working in a retail pharmacy, filling prescriptions for a couple of hours. It quickly became very busy and FlatScott had to jump in to help John get through the rush. Jelly appeared with what John was starting to believe was a permanent 24/7 smile. He felt this was truly a friendly, upright, and honest woman. She was so thoughtful, she would even come back every so often to see if either of them needed to be relieved for a fifteen-minute break.

They finally took her up on the offer, and John followed FlatScott back to the office. Jelly had previously poured each of them a cup of coffee and set out a few jelly donuts on a plate. She had known that her man would finally be ready for a break.

"My wife is such an exceptionally kind woman," FlatScott remarked.

John nodded in total agreement.

"Have you rid yourself of the rust from taking a break from retail pharmacy? Does it feel normal again?"

"The rust came off pretty quickly, actually," John said.

"Once a pharmacist, always a pharmacist," FlatScott assured.

****

FlatScott was on his second jelly donut and third cigarette when John very discretely asked him the question he'd been wondering all morning.

"Are any of the prescriptions I've been filling made up of pharmaceutical samples?"

"I'm sure, some of them, yes," he replied.

"Have samples been used in the promotion of pharmaceutical sales for a long time?" he asked.

FlatScott explained that as far back as he could remember, there had been samples involved in the marketing of pharmaceuticals. But representatives hadn't always left so many samples. Back in the day, reps would just leave a few.

At first, reps would leave just enough trial samples for a physician to give a few days' worth of doses at most. Then, physicians could see how the samples worked on those patients. Samples were also looked upon as a way for a patient to start a drug immediately while waiting to have their prescription filled at the pharmacy. If the patient had a side effect from the drug, then they would know not to have the prescription filled and to try something else.

"This all makes good sense to me," John said. "But now it seems like there is an abundance of samples for most brand-name products that reps leave at medical clinics."

"Thank goodness for that, John. It's a sweet situation for us. Everybody is a winner when it comes to samples. Well, almost. Physicians win because they're able to give a patient something tangible and valuable before the patient leaves their office. The patient feels like he's getting something for free. And the pharmaceutical companies feel this is a way to ensure they get patients on their products," said FlatScott.

"You said 'almost,' but you didn't say *why* 'almost.' Who loses?" John asked.

"Seasoned pharmacists will tell you that they lose. Most pharmacists believe that physicians abuse sample privileges. They think physicians help people who struggle financially, which may or may not be OK, but they are troubled that physicians also give out too many samples to patients who can fend for themselves and don't really need the help. So the physician either doesn't write a script at all, or writes a smaller script to be filled at the pharmacy. Because of this, the majority of retail pharmacists think they lose out on making as much profit as they should."

John told FlatScott that when he was in pharmacy school, he had heard a rumor that samples were going to fall by the wayside. In place of samples, there would be coupons and coupon books. Sample closets in clinics would become coupon closets and each coupon could be taken to a pharmacy and redeemed for the product in place of samples. That way, it would ensure that samples were not abused in any way and that the pharmacists could turn the coupons in to the manufacturers for redemption.

"Sounds like everybody would win with that kind of program!" John said.

FlatScott laughed and said, "You really are young and green! That coupon idea has been floating around for the past twenty-five years. It'll never happen. Congress and the FDA will never force that on the pharmaceutical companies. But between you and me, I've always believed that the system should work that way. If that were to occur, however, there would probably be a way for coupons to be abused as well. I personally hope, for selfish reasons, that they don't change the system."

The two sat in silence for a short time, reflecting on their conversation.

Finally, FlatScott asked, "Can you tell I was previously a pharmaceutical rep in my lifetime?"

After working in a retail pharmacy for five years, he had decided to try being a professional rep. He worked for a major pharmaceutical company for another five years and then left the position to start up his own retail pharmacy, RX Health.

John was about to ask how he got involved with Chuck, but before he could, Jelly stuck her head in the doorway and said, "Break's up, boys!"

FlatScott told John that they could talk again at lunch and that Ryan would be joining them at one o'clock to relieve John. He hoped that John could stay around to continue their conversation.

John would have stayed voluntarily. Time seemed to really be flying by filling prescriptions next to FlatScott, when Ryan arrived.

"The cavalry has arrived!" he announced. "You boys hungry?" he asked. He had picked up three large pizzas for the crew, including FlatScott's favorite: Canadian bacon, pineapple, and black olives. Ryan turned to John and exclaimed, "I just guessed your favorite pizza: muff pizza, right?"

John turned red and was glad Sara wasn't around to hear Ryan's nasty remark.

FlatScott and John shared the pizza in the office. John knew he couldn't stay long because FlatScott would soon be smoking, and the noxious fumes really did a number on his respiratory system. But before he left, FlatScott gave a few nice compliments.

"I'm impressed by your work today," he said. "You have a great future with Chalk Pharma, or even RX Health, if you want!" He told John that he was the president and founder of RX Health, and if John played his cards right, he might even take FlatScott's position after he retired.

John saw an opening where he could get some information, so he asked FlatScott what his relationship with the nursing homes involved.

FlatScott winked and said, "Legally, I have a contractual agreement with them."

With dismay, John realized that he had not found out anything for Jason, but at least he and FlatScott had a great rapport.

Before leaving, John decided, at the very least, to find out more of what was going to happen tonight. He asked FlatScott if he was going to give a PowerPoint presentation in his lecture.

"I'm only going to lecture, and I have to put something together this afternoon. Chuck called me at the last minute to be a speaker and I'm not too happy about the change, but Chuck felt everybody needed an update on this new competitor's product."

With that tidbit of information, John said his good-byes to everybody and left to rest before that evening's shindig.

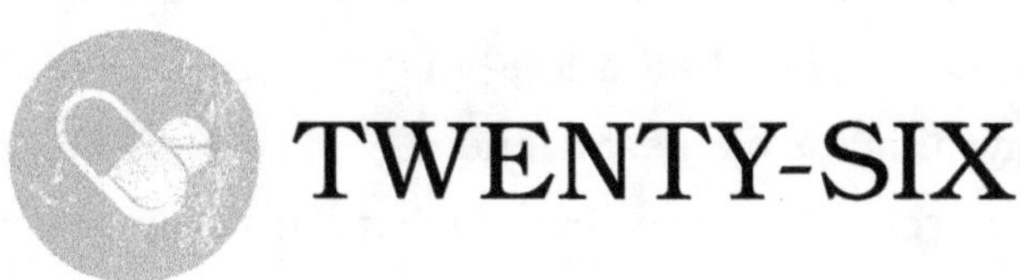# TWENTY-SIX

Greg was never one to sing—on any occasion—but as he lathered up in the shower in preparation for Shirley Phillips' arrival, he hummed the theme song to *Boogie Nights* and felt happier than ever. He rinsed himself and turned off the water, and just as he was reaching for a towel, he heard the phone ring.

Thinking it might be his lady friend, he quickly dried off his ears and answered. He was only slightly disappointed to hear John's voice instead of the sultry tones of Shirley Phillips.

"Where the hell are you?" John asked.

"Just getting out of the shower."

"What, have you been chasing puss all night?"

Greg started laughing and said, "Milkman, you would not believe the night I had. But, as I am a gentleman, I do not discuss my conquests. Even if I am a male slut."

Once they quit gibing each other, John reminded Greg that they were going to the gun shop to look at pistols next week. Greg said he believed he would have a hectic schedule between work and women, but he thought he'd still be able to fit it in.

When John got off the phone, he realized how much he enjoyed his friendship with Greg. He was one of those guys who could be a true gentleman, but at the same time, be one of the biggest, crudest pervs you've ever met—in a funny way, of course. One thing was for sure: They had a long history together, and John would do anything for his best friend.

Following his conversation with Greg, he left Sara a message to let her know that he was finished at RX Health and was heading home to rest before driving out to the farmhouse for the picnic. Moments after leaving the message, he received a call from Mavis.

"Don't forget to bring your basketball shoes. I'm looking forward to smoking you on the court," Mavis said.

"Yeah," John retorted, "a guy a foot taller smokes me in basketball, real fair. Bring it on, Big Man!"

"I can't wait to show you my famous windmill dunk!" Mavis yelled and abruptly hung up the phone.

****

Ann ran around her house making final preparations for the food and beverages she would serve at her husband's party that night. Earlier in the day, she had finished Chuck's list and, as she expected, he had told her not to worry about receipts. He barely even looked up from his computer. She wondered if he could even tell that she was in the best mood she'd been in for years. She hoped that if Chuck noticed her joy, then he would think it was because of the diamond necklace he had given her.

Chuck had purchased the meat for barbecuing the night before. He was an egotistical man by nature, but Chuck Frazier truly thought he made the best barbecue sauce in Kansas City. When Chuck got home from the butcher shop, Ann was at the kitchen counter washing vegetables. He playfully slapped her backside and nuzzled the back of her neck. "When we get back tonight from the picnic, maybe we can do a little *cow tipping*," he whispered. He then began to kiss along the path her diamond necklace made down her décolletage.

Ann shoved him away with her free hand and wondered what he meant by 'cow tipping.' She hoped she would never find out. Really, she wanted nothing more to do with this unsavory man. As she thought this, Chuck told her they would have to leave ninety minutes early to set up.

She listened to him laughing as he walked out of the kitchen. He must have thought his joke was pretty hilarious. To Ann, it was just further proof that he was a grade-A asshole. At least he'd noticed the diamond necklace. Maybe it had misled him into believing everything was fine and he would leave her alone so she could make plans to get out.

****

Miles away from the farm where he had been just a week earlier for his first shucking party, John realized again that he had never seen any video footage from the surveillance devices that were supposedly hidden there. It was unusual that Thorne's office hadn't shared any of the material with him or asked him any questions. It struck John that maybe there was no surveillance to see because the equipment had been removed from both the inside and outside of the farmhouse.

Maybe the mole in Jason's office had alerted Chuck and they had uprooted the devices.

He thought about how carefully the samples were handled. No one could see the actual samples themselves when they were taken outside to be transported, and if there was only outside surveillance, the footage would be of no consequence. John made a mental note to tell Greg about this and have him check with Jason. All of a sudden, a shiver ran up his spine, and he realized what a dangerous game he was in now.

John pulled over the car, got out, and raised the trunk. His coach gun was right where he had left it. He was relieved that he had decided not to take the company car, and had instead taken BD. He took the old-time shotgun and put it underneath a blanket in the backseat. It calmed his nerves; at least, it calmed him enough to drive the rest of the way to the farmhouse.

When he arrived, he saw that there was a tent set up to the side of the farmhouse, along with a large gas grill. Ann walked by herself toward the side door of the farmhouse. He couldn't blame Greg for his attraction; Ann was a beautiful woman. She was wearing skintight, navy-blue shorts and a blue midriff top that tied in the front. Once again, he found himself wondering why she had ended up with a slug like Chuck.

As he walked toward the tent, Ann heard his arrival and hollered, "Hi, John!"

He nodded and found the rest of the group sitting under the shade. Everyone was cordial, including a district member whom John had not yet met. His name was Paul Spencer and he looked to be in his mid-forties. After chatting with him for a short while, John discovered that he had a couple of kids in college. He had driven all the way from Wichita, which was where his territory was located.

Once their conversation had died down, John began to wonder who was running the show. Joe Arnold seemed to be in charge, even though he was one of the laziest reps John had ever met. Mike Currey was sitting close by and seemed to be his usual, carefree self. Mike was quite the politician when it came to Chuck. Mavis Turner was also present and made quite a sight to behold with his long legs folded up to sit in a small, plastic lawn chair.

Joe stood up and told the group that they were going to play basketball first. He named off the teams: himself, Paul, and the muff-pie chaser: John. Along with Chuck, the other team would be comprised of Ryan, Mike, and Mavis. The game was going to be three on three, with one reserve player on Chuck's team.

Ann appeared at the tent and started jumping up and down, asking if she could be the cheerleader for both squads. John watched the men's faces as she spoke. They all had a similar, hungry look, and it certainly wasn't for the barbecue.

The basketball hoop and backboard were just above the barn door. John was happy to see a brand-new net; he just loved the sound of a basketball swishing through fresh netting.

Chuck's team decided that Chuck and Paul would tag in and out for each other. Chuck started the game, and John wondered who would be the first to have a heart attack—Chuck or Ryan.

Ryan's team quickly went up by four points after Mavis made two uncontested slam dunks. At this juncture, Joe threw the ball to Chuck, but his Boss turned at the last minute, and the ball slammed into his face, breaking his sunglasses and giving him a bloody nose. It was a great feat for John to hold in his laughter, but he did.

Mike rushed over to see if Chuck was OK. Chuck threw his sunglasses to the side and said it was nothing. He refused to sub out for Paul and asked why they weren't playing. John admired the way Chuck handled the incident, which only made him sad once more about how much he had admired him when he'd netted the job out of pharmacy school.

The two squads played three games and Ryan's team won two out of the three. Of course, when you have a giant on your team, it is shameful not to win the majority of the games. Nevertheless, John congratulated his team and was satisfied by their efforts. He had played a good game and wished that Sara were there to see it.

With the conclusion of the games, Chuck finally began to fire up the barbecue grill and Ann brought out trays of food from the farmhouse. John helped Ann so she wouldn't have to make as many trips. Once inside the farmhouse, John was surprised when she asked him if he had talked to Greg lately.

"Um, yeah," he said.

"Did he mention me at all?" she asked. Her face looked so hopeful—like that of a child on Christmas—that he felt awful when he told her that Greg hadn't mentioned her.

"That funny boy," Ann said, and carried more food outside.

That horny boy, John thought.

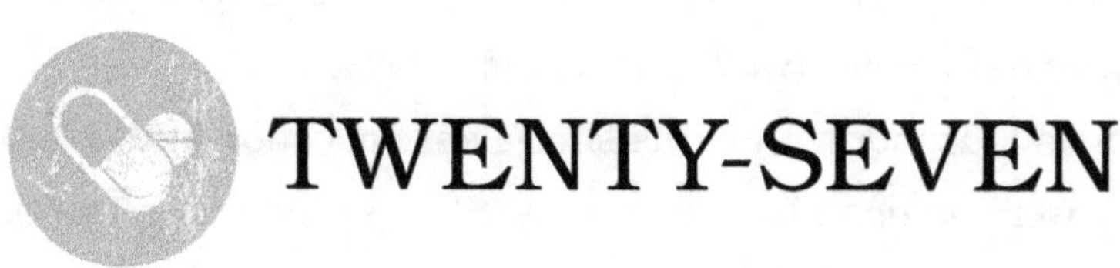# TWENTY-SEVEN

Greg's doorbell rang at nine o'clock on the dot. He had been preparing himself for the mental games that Shirley might decide to play, and took a deep breath before opening the door. He was greeted by a beautiful woman dressed in an all-white, formal evening gown. She was a knockout, and it took Greg a moment to realize that this was the same Shirley from the DA's office.

"Come in," Greg said, still flabbergasted by her beauty.

"I can see by the look on your face that you didn't expect me to come all dolled up."

She walked in and Greg noticed that she was carrying a large, brown grocery bag.

"Which way is the kitchen?" she asked.

Greg led her to the kitchen with a big grin on his face. She took two liquor bottles out of the bag, one was Crown Royal whiskey and the other was a chilled bottle of butterscotch schnapps that she had just picked up at her apartment before coming to Greg's. She asked Greg if he liked Finger-Me-Good shots.

"They're my favorite, so I brought fixings for them tonight," she explained.

Greg wordlessly pulled two shot glasses out of his cupboard.

"Got any more than two?" she asked.

He pulled four more out of his shot-glass collection and asked her if they were going to have company. She giggled and said no. She just liked to make a large batch at once so they could have them throughout the evening. Then she lined up all of the glasses and mixed six shots like a pro.

To Greg's delight, she downed two in a row before he had even finished his first. She proceeded to refill the empty glasses.

"Honey, do you have a tray to carry these shots to the living room?" she asked Greg.

Greg found one and quickly followed her with the shots. For the second night in a row, he found himself checking out a lady's behind. This one was just as sumptuous. He loved the way the formal dress clung to her curvaceous body.

Shirley and Greg sat together in the same spot that he and Ann had shared the night before. But in this case, Greg had no idea what kind of small talk he should start out with. Luckily, Shirley did the work for him and talked like a locomotive.

"I have a confession to make," she said.

"Oh yeah?" Greg asked, "Already starting to feel those shots?"

"I already knew that you liked Finger-Me-Good shots."

He laughed. "Does this mean you've been spying on me?" he asked.

"No," she said, "but I do know that when you're at the Pink Pussy Lounge, you favor these and chase them with a bottle of Michelob Light. I think it is cute that some of your shot glasses came from the Pink Pussy Lounge."

"What the hell? Who told you that I go to the Pink Pussy?" Rather than wait for her reply, he said, "Let me guess: You know someone who works there."

"Yeah, you're right," she said, but there was something about her voice that seemed less than enthused.

Greg went to the refrigerator and brought back a case of Michelob Light for chasers. Shirley kept on talking, and Greg noted how different she was from Ann. Ann had a certain *je ne sais quoi* that Shirley lacked, but Shirley had a self-assuredness that made him feel both uneasy and turned on at the same time.

Ann, on the other hand, was soft and tender. She needed a protector and Greg was happy to play the role. With a pang of regret, he thought about the special night they had shared and how much he cared for Ann, but one look at Shirley's plunging neckline quickly took his mind off of it.

Shirley told him about attending an eastern law school. Greg asked if she had to take out a lot of loans, and she said that she was debt-free. This puzzled Greg, since he had a rather sizeable amount of loan debt, as did most of his peers from law school.

Shirley noticed the confused look on his face, but before she could explain, she downed another shot and chugged half a bottle of beer. She was well on her way to being drunk, and Greg couldn't deny that he was pleased about this—as long as she didn't pass out on him.

"My parents died when my brother and I were in grade school," she explained. "But we were lucky. A very nice Caucasian man took us in and raised us like his own children. I can't imagine what would have become of us if it wasn't for this wonderful man."

"Is he still alive?" he asked.

Shirley nodded. "Yes, he is. And he paid for both my and my brother's, education."

She kept talking and the more her mouth ran, the more booze they both downed. Greg couldn't believe how much alcohol this woman could put away. He was starting to feel pretty tipsy himself, but didn't want to admit a lady could drink him under the table.

"Do you want to know my most embarrassing moment in law school?" Shirley asked.

"Why not?" he replied. But really, he was anxious to move past the talking. And she seemed to be almost there too. She leaned close to him and placed one of her hands on his leg.

"One time, I was sitting in my Torts Law class and the professor was discussing the concept of specific performance when my girlfriend leaned over and asked, 'Could a woman who promised a man a BJ be sued if she didn't perform the act?' I told my friend that it was probably so because that woman was the *only woman* who could perform it in that *exact manner*."

She explained that the two of them started laughing and the law professor came down hard on them. He asked Shirley to stand and tell the class what was so funny. She stood up and looked over at her friend, who had turned beet red, and said, "I'd better take the Fifth."

The professor refused. She had interrupted his discussion of an important legal concept and he wanted in on the joke. So she blurted out exactly what her friend had asked her. And to her relief, the professor started laughing hysterically.

Greg chuckled. "Sounds like your law classes were more fun than mine ever were. By the way, what was his answer?"

"He never answered!" she replied. "But I did get an A in that class."

With this, Shirley quickly stood up and announced that she had to pee. Greg pointed out the way to the bathroom. As he waited for her to return, in his inebriated state, he took a quick whiz in the potted plant in the living room. Greg had another shot and realized in his fuzzy state that he had made the right decision to not get a prescription for the blue pill. He could handle two women in two nights. Plus, he still had enough sense to know that he should not be taking any pill with the amount of alcohol he had consumed that evening.

Shirley came back to the living room, and Greg had to blink several times to be sure he wasn't imagining things. In front of him stood a knockout woman wearing only a pair of white panties and a lacy bra, along with her full-length, white evening gloves and high heels.

"I like white because it makes me feel like a virgin again," she said.

Greg just stared at her, mouth agape, and she asked him if he'd ever enjoyed a little chocolate before.

"Quite honestly," he replied, "I have not, but I've had a craving my entire life."

"Well you're in for a real treat, baby," Shirley slurred.

They headed for the bedroom and Shirley closed the door part way. Once inside the bedroom, Shirley removed the remaining articles of clothing, but left on her gloves.

"Aren't you going to take off the gloves?" he asked.

Shirley's words became more slurred the more she tried to speak.

"Don't you think they're sexy? I call these my *come-fuck-me gloves*."

After a long night of innuendo and booze, he simply couldn't contain himself any longer. He was so caught up in the moment that he didn't even bother to shut the door the rest of the way before switching off the lights and pouncing on her.

****

Greg lay beside Shirley, spent and panting, and wondered if this was what heaven was like. Two beautiful women in two days—Greg couldn't believe his luck. Just the same, he couldn't help but acknowledge the nagging voice in the back of his mind, reminding him of the silent vow he had made to Ann the night before. But Ann would never know about this playful romp so she would not be harmed.

His thoughts were suddenly interrupted by a low, raspy voice.

"Sis, it sounded like you really enjoyed that action."

Greg knew that it wasn't Shirley speaking, but the room was too dark to make out any other figures. He gathered the sheets around him and sat up, just as the intruder flicked on the overhead light and he finally saw who it was.

"Son of a bitch!" Greg yelled.

Standing at the foot of his bed was none other than Belle, Simple Simon's creepy nurse. She was wearing a black jumpsuit and matching gloves, and the outfit only confounded Greg more. He had no idea why this woman was at the foot of his bed, but Shirley soon cleared that up.

"Greg," she said, "I'd like you to meet my brother."

Greg turned to Shirley and saw that she had slipped out of bed and was now pointing a small, semiautomatic .380 pistol directly at him.

"What the hell are you doing with that? And what do you mean that's your *brother?*" he demanded.

Shirley started laughing, and Belle joined in. Together, they made up the most maniacal duet of laughter that Greg had ever heard.

"Well, *sweetheart,*" she began, "the mystery man who took me and my brother in is pretty well known around these parts. I'm sure you've heard of him: Simple Simon?"

Greg couldn't believe what he was hearing. This woman had completely tricked him. His mind raced as he tried to think of what else she could have been up to.

As if reading his thoughts, Shirley said, "Yes, I have been the snitch in Jason's office since day one. Now I think it's time for Belle to disclose the rest of the mystery."

Slowly and deliberately, Belle unzipped the front of her jumpsuit all the way to the crotch. For a split second, Greg felt like he was back at the Pink Pussy, but when his eyes reached Belle's nether region, he couldn't believe what he saw.

"You're a fucking *tranny!*" he exclaimed.

Now the two really roared with laughter.

Greg realized that the only thing left was for him to face the music. But he wasn't going down without a fight. He grabbed a pillow and threw it at the gun in Shirley's hand. The pistol flew up and Greg simultaneously jumped out of bed and reached for his Colt. All he felt was empty space! He had forgotten to put the gun back after the cleaning lady had left the day before, which meant that both guns were locked away in his car.

Before he could curse himself any more for his stupid mistake, Belle grabbed him from behind, picked him up, and snapped his neck. When it was done, she deposited him back onto the floor, now a limp, lifeless body.

"Glad that wasn't messy," Shirley said as she slipped back into her clothes.

Once she was dressed, Belle told her to remove the sheets and pillowcases so the authorities couldn't scan them for bodily fluids or hair. They had taken precautions to not leave any fingerprints on the furniture by both wearing gloves, as planned. By the time they were done, they had sanitized the place so there would be no trace of them.

Shirley looked over Greg's dead corpse.

"Thanks for the lovely evening," she sneered.

She joined her brother in the living room and together they gathered the empty beer bottles, shot glasses, and partially empty liquor bottles, tossing them into a large brown bag. Before they walked out the door, Belle, with a smile, grabbed the last of the beer bottles that remained unopened in the case and looked forward to out-drinking her sister once they left the apartment. The two then quietly slipped out, unnoticed.

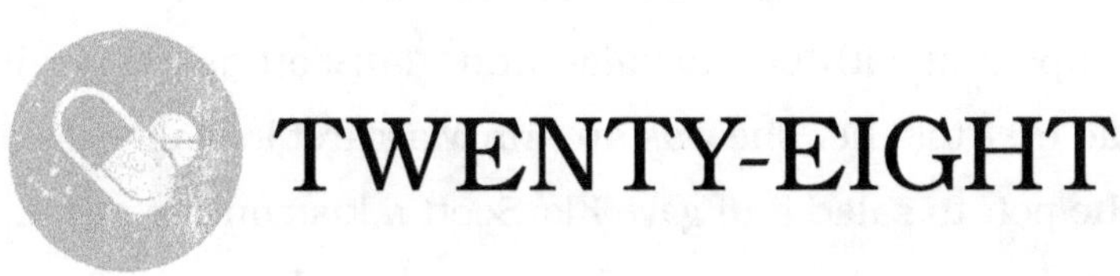

TWENTY-EIGHT

"Pick your barbecue protein, boys. Steak or pork chops," Chuck called out as the group walked over to the grill area. He started to serve up the meat when he heard a horn out front.

It was FlatScott in his family station wagon. He parked the car and joined the rest of the gang, who started filling him in on the game he had missed.

"You should have been here, man. Then the teams would have been even," Ryan said. "I would have played such tight defense on you, you would have thought I was trying to squeeze into your Fruit of the Looms."

"Keep it up, and you'll have to take a test after my lecture tonight," FlatScott teased. "And I have a funny feeling you won't fare well."

John watched this comical exchange with amusement. He had never seen FlatScott out of work clothes, and he just looked funny in his shorts, T-shirt, and sneakers. The outfit really emphasized his knobby knees and hairless legs.

"I see you're still shaving your legs," Joe Arnold pointed out. FlatScott shook his fist at him.

John thought that Joe was too much of a smartass for his own good, but he was close to Chuck and could get away with anything, so long as he knew when to kiss ass.

Ann reappeared with potato salad and FlatScott asked her if anybody had ever told her she was an Ann Margaret lookalike. She set down the potato salad and gave FlatScott a kiss on the cheek.

"You're just a sweetie pie," she lovingly replied.

"Hey, if you ever get tired of your old man, just let me know," FlatScott joked.

"I'm not sure Jelly would take to that idea," she said.

John watched Chuck overhear this conversation, and was impressed when Chuck just smiled and otherwise showed no reaction. Once again, he thought about Greg. If Greg had heard a remark like that, then he would have most definitely reacted. Greg would want to be the only man commenting on Ann's looks, that's for sure.

****

By the time the group had finished their meal, it was time to go into the house where FlatScott would make his presentation in the living room. John felt sorry for Ann. She was the only one left to clean up the tremendous mess they had made while stuffing themselves with barbecue. The rest of the group watched and listened to the lecture while polishing off more beer.

John wondered if there was any surveillance equipment in the house. He had the feeling that there was probably none and he suddenly felt very alone. Here he was, sitting in a room filled with criminals involved in the shucking scheme, and he was the one who was going to bring it all down. He was the rat. And now there was a mole in Jason Thorne's office. There was no telling what these men actually knew.

Further into FlatScott's lecture, John noticed that Chuck had brought Ann into the living room, and they sat together holding hands. Ann looked rather dejected, but he did notice that she had a dazzling diamond necklace around her neck. She must have had it tucked under her top earlier so that nothing got on it. Between the ice around her neck, and the rock on her finger, she was wearing a small fortune.

****

As the group sat comfortably around the living room, everybody tried to listen intently to the lecture through the beer and barbecue halo. Little did they know that as they enjoyed FlatScott's presentation, three horseback riders had arrived at the barn.

The riders dismounted and tied up their quarter horses inside the barn, making sure that the barn door was closed behind them. It was obvious that these men were riding extremely good horseflesh. One of the horses was a very nice-looking bay quarter horse stallion with a glossy, black mane and long, black tail. It had the classic black coloring that started at the top of its hoofs and ran up its legs. The other two horses—one a sorrel stallion, and the other a grulla stallion—were also very well-bred quarter horses, and like the bay, had a great deal of athletic ability.

To complete the picture, the men were dressed in black Western wear, including boots, cowboy hats, and gloves. In fact, two of the three had worn the same shirts and pants one murderous night not too long ago in the Ozarks. This was not out of the ordinary for the area, as a lot of the people who lived out in the country rode horses. These three definitely looked like they had ridden out of the pages of history.

The leader of the group was one of the same capos who'd had breakfast earlier in the week at Simple Simon's. He told the two members of his crew to relax. At eleven o'clock exactly, the party would break up and they would see Chuck leave to get more beer for the ones who would make up the cleanup crew. Chuck's departure would be the signal for them to move in.

At this moment, all three men reached into a saddlebag that was on the capo's bay quarter horse, and each pulled out his own gun. These were no ordinary guns; these were the new kind of pistols that Simple Simon wanted all his men to have. The capo made sure that his would be used as a .45 and that the two soldiers had theirs loaded with .410 shotgun shells.

****

Shortly before eleven, Chuck dismissed everyone inside the house. He told everyone to drive safely and went on to joke, "All right, scholars, time to go back to your own palaces."

When they started clearing out, Chuck said, "Except for you two. FlatScott and John, you both are on cleanup detail with Ann. I'm going to run out and get some more beer and some coffee for anyone who needs it."

Before they had a chance to reply, Chuck was out of the house.

Now that John was alone with FlatScott and Ann, he began to think more about his buddy Greg. Once again he was thinking how he had missed not going out as much as he had hoped to with Greg, but he wasn't going to let their friendship fall by the wayside.

He planned to strike more of a balance with his free time so that he could spend more time with Greg, not just Sara. After all, Greg had always been loyal, not to mention that he was helping him with the worst ordeal he'd ever experienced. Plus, he also probably would become rich from this whole mess and he wanted to make sure his good friend reaped some financial reward from it as well.

****

Once Chuck had driven away from the farmhouse, the three men inside the barn opened the barn door slightly and slid through it. They then began approaching the farmhouse. One of the soldiers entered through the back door that led into the kitchen, and simultaneously, the other soldier and the capo came through the front door that Chuck had purposely left unlocked.

Ann, who happened to be in the kitchen when the enforcer appeared, let out a terrific scream.

He grabbed Ann around the neck, called her *sweet ass*, and dragged her into the living room. The capo then ordered FlatScott and John to sit down on the chairs at the table in the dining room. The enforcer placed Ann in an empty chair as well as around the table. FlatScott just kept hollering, "What the hell is going on?"

All three of these men kept their newly acquired guns in their hands throughout this ordeal. John was in a state of shock, but finally realized what was going on. He kept thinking he needed to get to his coach gun that was in the backseat of his car.

The enforcer roughly grabbed one of Ann's breasts while he was standing behind her chair. Immediately, the capo told him to take his "damn hand" off of Ann. John and FlatScott were both relieved to hear that.

The capo told his crew members, "Don't forget: Simple Simon doesn't want any of these people violated. After all, we are very humanitarian."

The enforcer who had grabbed Ann had a confused look on his face, like he did not know what the capo meant. At this point, John knew for sure that these low-life scumbags were sent by Simple Simon—and probably Chuck too!

FlatScott told them they were making a huge mistake and that Chuck should be back anytime and would straighten this whole mess out. The three men just howled and laughed.

The capo told FlatScott that he was an idiot and that he had nothing to worry about. FlatScott leaned back in his chair with relief. Between the capo saying they were not to be violated and telling him he had nothing to worry about, he felt more at ease.

Suddenly, the capo raised his revolver and fired one direct shot into the middle of FlatScott's forehead. It knocked FlatScott onto the floor and blood began pouring out profusely.

Ann began crying hysterically as John hollered, "You asshole! You told him he had nothing to worry about!"

With a big smile on his face, the capo said in a calm voice, "He didn't. It was quick and his family will be able to have an open casket because he was hit with just one slug."

In the middle of all this hysteria, the enforcer by Ann began fondling her breast again.

The capo pointed his pistol at him and said, "Stop playing with her tits. If it were up to me, I'd let you do whatever you want, but it's not my decision."

"Come on, just gimme fifteen minutes alone with her," the enforcer begged.

The other enforcer finally spoke up and said, "Yeah, what would it hurt if the two of us take fifteen minutes to do things to her that Chuck would never even dream of?"

"You two morons are always thinking with the wrong head. You never want to cross Simple Simon. Remember, we are only supposed to make this look like a robbery," the capo replied.

With this, the capo reached over and grabbed the diamond necklace that Chuck had just given Ann, yanking it forcibly from her neck. Then he grabbed her left hand and pulled the expensive diamond wedding ring off her finger.

At this moment, John tried to get out of his chair and grabbed at the capo. He was hit from behind by the butt of the pistol of the enforcer who was beside him. He was then thrown back into his chair, now in a semi-conscious state.

The capo told his two enforcers, "Go ahead; get it over with."

With that, the enforcer beside Ann said to her, "You're going to join Greg now, sweet ass."

He shot Ann point-blank in the back of her head with his pistol, which had the shotgun shells in it. Some of Ann's brain, body tissue and blood splattered onto John, covering the front of his chest and head.

While Ann lay dead on the floor, the enforcer said, "Chuck did not want you in an open casket, bitch."

As John returned to full consciousness, he heard the capo say to him, "A son-of-a-bitch snitch like you only deserves the worst."

The other enforcer quickly forced his loaded shotgun shell pistol into John's mouth and squeezed the trigger. Before it went off, just before the thunderous explosion when his thoughts were blasted apart into a million pieces, the last image John had was of Sara and the way she had looked when he told her he wanted to share his life with her.

The dark riders put their guns away and mounted their horses once more. They rode off into the night, knowing that this wasn't their first rodeo and it wouldn't be their last. So long as Simple Simon ran the show, they knew that they would come back again and again for one more curtain call. Coincidentally, these murderers looked a lot like the gang in the framed print hanging behind the bar in the farmhouse.

****

On the seventieth anniversary of the Union Station Massacre, the outfit was now responsible for the deaths of four people in the Kansas City area. The mob's pharmaceuticals-diversion enterprise was still safely utilizing the three-legged-stool strategy. Consequently, the mob's profits from this part of their business would continue to help fuel their existence and more scourge on society!